THE
VEGAN
REVOLUTION
... WITH ZOMBIES

DAVID AGRANOFF

DEADITE PRESS

deadite
press

205 NE BRYANT
PORTLAND, OR 97217

AN ERASERHEAD PRESS COMPANY
WWW.ERASERHEADPRESS.COM

ISBN: 1-936383-13-6

Acknowledgements: Thank you Carlton, you knew before I did that I had to write this book. The staff at Eraserhead for supporting this project. The staff at the Vegan mini-mall for talking to me about their post-zombie apocalypse plans and letting me film the trailer at their spot. Tim Khan for making the trailer happen, seriously that was awesome! Rat for doing the music for the trailer. Nicole, Jeff, and all the zombies who showed up to be in the trailer. Try Vegan PDX for doing what it does. Every work I do requires the love and support of my partner, Cari, who is the best rabbit momma ever. My work-out partner, Ed, who deals with me when I am still in novel land when my head should be at the gym. Karen at Afterbirth. Magik. Bru-Dawg. Paul my most trusted reader. Thanks in advance to anyone who spreads the word about the book.

For Karl,

Without his words you may not be holding this book.

Tag you're it!

"One plus one is how it's won"
—Insted

For Immediate Release:

From Senator Tom Harkrat (Iowa - D)

Many observers on Capital Hill are already aware of today's groundbreaking advancement in genetic engineering announced by Vir-Tech Industries. Senator Harkrat has long been a supporter of Vir-Tech and even co-sponsored, with Republican Senator Ron Pence of Indiana, the bill that secured their funding. This advancement in biotechnology ends the debate over the harsh and cruel treatment of livestock forever. It ensures that the nutritional demands of our growing population can be balanced with a concern for a painless existence for farm animals.

The neuroscientists at Vir-Tech have found that by destroying a laboratory rat's cingulate cortex, or by injecting the rat with morphine, they can block its perception of pain. Recently, their scientists have learned to genetically engineer animals so that they lack certain proteins that are important to the operation of the anterior cingulate cortex.

Over the next three months, animals engineered to never experience pain will be entering the American food supply. That's not all: Vir-Tech has extended its research to dampen the centers of the recently discovered duruagate cortex. This is center of the brain's activity in relation to boredom, abandonment and stress. This will provide a stress-free life for livestock producing things like dairy products, eggs and wool, to name a few industries active in Senator Harkrat's state.

The Stress-Free Animal Act was supported by a bi-partisan vote and has found unlikely allies, such as ethics professor Peter Sangar, the father of the animal rights movement, and the Humane Society of the United States. They have already applauded the work of Vir-tech. A joint statement with the Beef and Dairy Councils is expected from a coalition of animal welfare organizations in the morning. We hope members of the media will join Senator Harkrat for his famous BBQ ribs at the Capitol. He'll be serving the first ribs made from the Stress-Free animal label, produced in Butte, Iowa.

Prologue

Really, who hasn't dreamed of shooting yuppies?

Dani stood through the sunroof of the Toyota Prius and loaded another shell into the chamber of the shotgun. *Who says you can't make your dreams come true?*

Only a few months ago this had been nothing but a psychotic fantasy. The woman walking toward Dani had been an upper class snob, drinking only the finest wine at art walks and seeing only independent or Oscar-worthy films; a true asshole who never left Portland's yuppie condo zone of the Pearl District.

Now, months after the world fell apart, this same woman looked dirtier than a crust punk after a hundred-band fest in July. Her designer clothes from Nordstrom's rack were soiled by the people whose brains she had eaten days ago. She had a harem of skeeters and fruit flies colonizing an open wound on her neck. She may have been yuppie at one time; now, she was just a zombie.

"Do it!" Mark yelled from the driver's seat.

Dani lowered the shotgun, targeting the yuppie woman's rotting purple head. The sound of the shotgun blast echoed against the high-rise condos. Direct hit. The head disintegrated into flying mush and sprayed along the side walk. The headless zombie collapsed. Dani lowered the shotgun into the car and put her hand out. Mark lifted the AK-47 into her hands. She had never held a gun in her life before this week; now she couldn't believe the fun she had missed out on.

9

Dani had always found dancing, long bike rides and hard cardio workouts to be great stress relief. But that was nothing compared to the cathartic release of turning the masses that drove her nuts on the public buses a few months ago into mush. This was an addictive task for a well-educated misanthrope.

"Come on you fucking slime-bags, fresh meat."

Dani yelled at the building even though she knew they couldn't understand her. Brain bits and the sound of that first blast were not enough to bring on the flesh-eating hordes. Dani understood she just had to stand there, living bait. Mark clicked on his radio.

"Hey we have zombie bait down in the Pearl, request backup."

"Roger that," the voice came back and was followed by laughter. Everyone seemed amused by Mark's need to talk over the radios like he was a in a war movie. It's not that he had a military or law enforcement background. He just watched too many action movies. Sometimes he blasted the score to *Rambo: First Blood Part II* when they were driving in the remaining zombie zones.

The low groan of the zombies inside the lobby of the high-rise signaled their approach. Most of the zombies would rot up in those towers, destroying the expensive furniture with gray stained piles of broken-down zombie mush over the years to come. Very few figured out the stairs, and elevators, thankfully, were not in the zombie skill set. That meant the survivors only had to focus their attention on the lowest levels.

They chose this building because it had an easy-to-open revolving door. Four zombies pushed at the door. After the first one shambled out, the door smacked into the second zombie. The last three fell like dominoes back into the lobby.

"Ah, negative on that backup, it's under control." Mark looked up at Dani. Her focus was tight on the zombie walking toward her. It wasn't moving fast, dragging one foot like most of them did. This guy was not as purple and decayed as most.

"Oh man, this guy wants his brains."

Dani jumped up onto the roof of the car and then onto the sidewalk. The zombie turned to follow her. Dani sprayed AK fire over her shoulder without looking. Sure, she wasted a few rounds in the dude's chest, but his head went *pop*. She spun the door to the condo building, knocking more zombies into a pile. The domino zombies bit at the zombie on top of them like a cannibal train. The top zombie groaned but didn't have the strength to stand. Zombies could eat other zombies, but it was like eating white bread, meaningless carbs. They had to eat the living to continue to do whatever it is they do.

Dani put her foot on the door to push it open and squeezed her AK.

"Wait!" said a voice; the sound was like a needle scratching across a full length LP. Dani turned around and saw Samantha of the Abolitionist Voice Committee. "Don't shoot Dani!"

"I am so not in the mood for an ideological discussion right now."

"If we intend to create a new world, we have to leave behind the madness of the old."

Dani watched over her shoulder as Mark marched toward them.

"Sam, I don't think we have much of choice about that whole 'leaving the old world behind' thing."

"We're vegans, and we need to find a nonviolent solution, as the professor once said..."

"Goddamn it Sam!" Mark yelled as he marched toward them. "Why don't you protest those PETA humane death camps and leave us alone."

"I admit," Samantha turned to address Mark, "the moral benchmark is a little grayer since . . ."

"Since the dead started walking and eating people's brains," Dani said. She pushed the door open and sprayed machine gun fire into the lobby of the building. The top zombie shredded into zombie crumbles before the two underneath stopped squirming. Samantha screamed, Mark laughed and Dani closed her eyes. She should have enjoyed this, you know, shooting yuppies.

Samantha cried and pointed. "They were people, just like you once."

"Yeah well, I changed in time." Dani slung the rifle over her shoulder and walked beside Mark toward their car.

"What happened to compassion? What happened to you, Dani?"

TEST

Feel free to write your answers in the book.

1. Government funding of research into eliminating the pain receptors of farmed animals was co-sponsored by:

      A) Senator Tom Harkrat

      B) A bunch of assholes

      C) Senator Ron Pence

      D) All of the above

2. Zombies continue to survive by:

      A) Eating lots of beans

      B) Eating vegetables

      C) Eating the flesh and brains of non-human animals

      D) Eating the brains of Weird Al Yankovic or Bob Barker

Chapter One

Six months ago ...

"George says we're going to have alfalfa for the rabbits."
"What rabbits?"
"We're gonna have rabbits an' a berry patch."
"You're nuts."
"We are too. You ast George."
"You're nuts." Crooks was scornful. "I've seen hundreds of zombies come by on the road an' on the ranches ..."

The stupidity of it all was overwhelming. Dani put the papers back in her folder and slammed it shut as if they might jump back out. She looked at her watch. It was almost six and Magik was late again. The brew pub was already full and she was tired of stopping people from borrowing the chairs at her table.

Dani leaned over to look out the window to the parking lot. Magik rolled up on his bike, but all twenty spots on the various bike racks were loaded with fixie bikes. Some of the bike seats and pedals were five feet in the air, and most had ridiculously short handle bars. She watched as he looked around and took a deep breath. The Mooch Lounge was a popular brew pub during indie rock shows, but she hadn't expected a crowd on a Monday night.

The smell of bacon and sweat coated the crowd, thick with

hipsters in a bizarre mating ritual. The men wore ringer T-shirts a size too small that displayed non sequiturs like the Sioux City YMCA or something equally ironic. It took her a moment to realize it, but almost all of them had handlebar mustaches. The women wore multi-colored knee socks sticking out of their tall second hand western boots, and most them had on oversized sunglasses despite being inside the darkened pub.

It wasn't until Dani's eyes followed a stinky plate of bacon in a server's hand that she saw the banner on the wall.

Mooch's Handlebar Mustache and Bacon Night – Mondays!

Magik set his messenger bag on the table and let out a sigh. "You know they charged me a cover because I don't have a mustache?"

Dani pointed at the banner.

"Last Monday at the Mooch!" said Magik as he kissed her on the forehead and sat down.

"So how was it?"

"The stout or the new job?"

"The job!"

Dani didn't want to answer. She and Magik had only dated for six months, but today was the first day of it that she had earned a penny. She had left New York eight months ago, ready for a new life on the west coast, and had no idea how hard it would be to find a job with her English degrees. She'd planned on editing tech journals or teaching fourth grade English, but the job market was harder in Portland than she imagined. Worse, Dani felt pressure to like the job at Fulci House Press, because it was a friend of Magik's who found it for her.

"Well, it's an editing job."

"Awesome," Magik put out his arms for a hug. He was so tall that he loomed over her even when sitting. His Viking-like features and questionable Nordic heritage ensured a yearly Thor costume on Halloween and occasional kinky evenings.

Dani looked away.

"No sweetie, it's editing, but they kinda lied in the interviews. They said I would be working on new editions of classic literature."

"Well, yeah," Magik pointed at a beer on the menu as their server passed the table. "Classic literature sure, but it's with zombies."

Dani's jaw almost dropped. "You already knew that!"

Magik looked around and back at Dani. She looked at him like he just clubbed a baby seal in Canada. "Hey now, you said you wanted an editing job--well, I found you one."

Dani opened her folder and slid the pages in front of Magik. "My first assignment."

Magik picked up the papers and smiled. "*Of Mice and Men . . .* cool."

"No, not *Of Mice and Men.* It's *Of Mice and Men with Zombies.* Written by Steinbeck and hacked apart by some fucking horror writer whose only other credit is *Raptor Attack III* for the SyFy Channel."

Magik stroked his goatee. "Did he write the whole trilogy or just part three?"

"It doesn't matter."

"It really does matter because *Raptor Attack II* was pretty good. It was like *Vertigo . . .* with dinosaurs. Could have been cooler if *Rear Window* with giant bugs hadn't been done in *Mimic Three.*"

Dani sighed. "The point is that they have taken a classic of literature, a statement about friendship in the face of great social injustice, and turned it into a book about fucking zombies."

"It's not that big a stretch really . . ."

"It's Steinbeck and brain-eating zombies."

"Romero is kinda like a Steinbeck."

"Who?"

Magik put his left hand over his eyes. "George A. Romero is Father, Son and Holy Fucking Ghost of the zombie genre. Director of its finest films. He set the rules, the whole thing. And look, Steinbeck wrote a trilogy of novels pointing to depression-era exploitation of the workers, right?"

"Sure."

"Well, Romero's original trilogy, I'm talking the first three, were social commentary for their times. Each one was made in a decade, which the film was basically about. We should watch them. I have all of his zombie movies at home."

The server dropped Magik's beer on the table and kept going, just as a man stopped at the table and pointed at Magik. "Magik, dude, no way."

The man wore a faded ringer T-shirt (for the Ben Franklin Thread and Needle Emporium in Warsaw, Indiana) that was so small his belly poked out of the bottom. The man pulled a chair forward and introduced himself but Dani couldn't hear the name over his wickedly curled mustache. "Can I join you? I just ordered a plate of bacon," said Mustache.

"Yeah man, cool, join us, we're celebrating. Dani just started a new job at Fulci House Press."

"Yeah, no shit?" Mustache seemed excited, as best Dani could tell considering his lips were MIA.

"So yeah, I am pretty sure Swayze could realistically take on the Red Army, taking in to consideration the Wolverines and the fact it was Swayze in his prime."

Dani sighed as she realized the conversation was hijacked. Magik was like clockwork; when conversations ground to a halt, or he nervously wanted to change the subject, he had a secret reserve of random statements. Conversation changers that could not be ignored.

"We're talking *Red Dawn* Swayze?" Speech escaped as the curled mustache moved up and down.

Dani couldn't expect more from Magik. She met him because he was the only person closer to the front of the line than her at a theater screening of *Battlestar Galactica* episodes featuring a live appearance and Q&A with Katee Sackhoff. Dani was there because of a pseudo-lesbian crush on Starbuck. Magik was there as a devoted geek. She thought he was cute and wanted to break the ice so she asked him an ice breaking question.

"I'm Dani. What is your name and tell me something interesting about yourself."

"I'm Magik, and I have had seventeen near death experiences."

It wasn't automatic love, but she was smitten when he saved a spot for her in the line for the next episode. Now back in the Mooch she gave him a look, and a non-farting silent but deadly communication passed between them. It may have been too soon in their courtship, but Dani hoped he would pick up the cue and ask Mustache to give them some privacy.

"Or *Steel Dawn* Swayze," Magik wiped frothy brew from his top lip. "What the fuck did you think I meant? *Ghost* Swayze?"

The two men laughed. Dani couldn't listen to this and she stared out the window. A group had gathered between the bike racks with their backs to the restaurant. It wasn't uncommon for the Mooch to be so full that even in the winter people would stand outside waiting to get in, but these people held up signs. Dani's attention was disrupted again as a foul smell came closer. The server walked over to their table and set down a steaming plate of bacon. The grease still bubbled on the wrinkled flesh. Mustache fanned the steaming pile with his napkin. It wasn't long before his face opened under the mustache and revealed a mouth watering for the bacon.

It wasn't like Dani was a vegetarian, she had eaten chicken for lunch, but the smell, mustache and bacon combo turned her stomach. She turned away and this time one of the protesters turned around. The sign proclaimed in blood red letters, *Meat is Murder.*

"You see that?" Dani pointed outside. Magik chewed lazily on a piece of bacon.

"Whatever." The mustache moved slightly around the hipster's face, similar to a non-mustached person when they chewed on food. "Whatever, it's organic and local."

Dani tipped the plate up.

"The bacon is local?"

"Yeah the farmers treat the animals super nice."

"Before they turn them into bacon?"

Mustache looked at Magik, who put down the bacon he held. Magik tried to wipe the grease off his fingers. Dani squirmed in her seat. The smell felt oppressive, like the air was becoming a solid greasy brick rolling between the hipsters and filling the empty spaces in the room with creamy lard. Dani knew it was in her mind, but watching the bacon disappear under the curled 'stache was nauseating.

"Come on man, bacon is like meat candy." Mustache hipster spoke with a full mouth. Pieces of crispy fat broke apart between his lips.

Dani pushed the plate of bacon toward him. "It's more like a bowl of ass shavings."

Magik leaned back in his chair; he didn't like the tone of this conversation. It was time for one of his game changing conversation bombs. He was like pitcher winding up to throw a deadly fast ball.

"So I'm not sure you're all aware that the Klingon language doesn't have a word for tear."

Strike one.

"Really," Mustache shook his head. "Do they have a word for leopard?"

"Good question," Magik pulled out his iPhone "I have an app for that."

Strike two.

"You ever see that TV show *Small Wonder?*" asked Mustache.

"Yeah, it was like a robot *Punky Brewster.*" Magik said laughing.

Strike three – you're out.

Dani slid her chair across the floor with a loud squeal and chugged the last of her beer.

"I need to get some fresh air," Dani said. She grabbed her coat.

Magik stood up, their eyes locked. Magik finally read her less-than-subtle cues. "Yeah, maybe we should be getting back to the house."

Dani looked around the room as she put her coat over her shoulder. The smell of the bacon felt like a solid barrier between her and the front door. It was like the pre-smoking ban stench that she would smell on her clothes long after they escaped. The hipsters didn't seem to mind. Several reached into their bowls greedily eating the last tiny bits of crispy pig with their fingers. One had a bowl tipped up to his mouth draining grease. His friends laughed at his ironic glory; they were all young enough that no doctor had told them to get their LDL numbers down – so fuck it, what is drinking a little bacon grease if it amuses the fellas. Dani shook her head at the display.

Dani pushed her way through the crowd and Magik fought to catch up to her. A group of young drunken frat-type looking guys knocked on the window to get the attention of the protesters. They wanted the protesters to witness them eating their bacon. One of them humped the air for no apparent reason, as he slowly lowered the blood red and gray ass-shaving into his mouth.

The brisk, fresh, un-bacon polluted air of the Pacific Northwest greeted Dani like an old friend, an old friend who didn't smell like shit. Dani put on her bike helmet as Magik stumbled out the door.

"Excuse me, would you like some information about the cruel treatment of animals?" Dani turned. A woman just shorter than her held out a leaflet that was about a third of page. "We are doing a screening of a ground breaking documentary called *Earthlings* with Joaquin Phoenix, perhaps you've heard of it?"

Dani looked at the flyer, It had the actor's face and a cow on it. Dani looked at the small group of activists. Only about four of them stood there. It had seemed like more a few minutes ago. The woman looked young but her friends holding the signs didn't. One of them was an older woman; another was a middle-aged looking man. Dani smiled at the young woman, she looked impossibly young but must have at least been old enough to get into the bar.

"Ok, this place is lame, but when I was your age, which was not that long ago, I spent every free night at a place like this." Dani held up the leaflet. "Why all this?"

Dani pointed at the small protest. The young activist nodded.

"Well, it's really foul that bacon has become so cool. Pigs are intelligent beings, and each piece of bacon represents suffering and murder. Someone said to me once, if it's murder in my head, I need to act like it's murder in my heart."

Dani lifted an eyebrow. It was simple but profound, said sweetly with an idealistic young voice. It was simple, but it hit Dani hard like a cast iron frying pan.

"Ready, sweetie?" Magik said, already on his bike. Dani hadn't even unlocked hers. Dani ignored Magik and smiled at the activist.

"That makes a lot of sense."

"Here," the activist smiled as she reached into her messenger bag and handed Dani a pamphlet. Dani looked at the title, *Why Vegan?* "You should read it, but also go see *Earthlings*, it's the reason I became vegan."

Dani smiled, as she had friends in college who were vegan. She had a feeling that it was a good thing to be, but she just couldn't imagine a life without eating a cheese pizza or scrambling eggs from time to time. Her heart still reeled from what the woman had said earlier. Dani smiled and put the pamphlet in her bag. "I'll check it out."

Dani walked toward her bike and Magik rolled up beside her. "So why don't I show you what a zombie movie is like."

TEST

1: Which actor did not stop an invading Communist army in a film made during the '80s?

    A) Chuck Norris

    B) Patrick Swayze

C) *David Hasselhoff*
D) *Lea Thompson*

2: *Bacon is:*
    A) A vegetable.
    B) Cholesterol-free
    C) A health food
    D) A shriveled greasy fat laden piece of a burnt corpse sliced off the belly or ass of a pig

Chapter Two

The bike ride home was quiet, for Dani anyway. As they pulled into Magik's driveway and pushed their bikes past his often ignored and unloved Volvo, she was still thinking about what the young activist had said.

Magik lived on the Southeast line between a nice family neighborhood and the section of the city referred to as Felony Flats. It wasn't the nicest part of town, but he could afford it and had set up a print shop in his basement. He printed t-shirts in the morning and worked on his long-in-development graphic novel in the afternoons. He wasn't rich but he didn't have to wear a suit every day and that was most important to him.

The only problem was his neighbors. Well really it wasn't the Harrisons, who'd lived in the house since 1974. It was their youngest son, Billy, who moved back into their basement after his third kid was born. That was very much a problem. As they dismounted their bikes, Dani almost jumped out of her skin. A fat man sat on the porch, his face painted white with a black clown smile. Smoke rose slowly from his face.

"'Sup Ninja?" Billy nodded and his enormous flesh ocean rolled like waves under his dirty Insane Clown Posse hoodie. Billy referred to himself as a Juggalo. Dani had no idea what that meant and it took Google to explain it to her. After twenty minutes of reading, and a couple of videos, Dani determined they were the most moronic youth subculture she had ever discovered. They dressed like clowns and listened to extremely lame hip hop with lyrics about violence and misogyny.

Magik nodded at his neighbor, who spent the summer shirtless with his pants hanging almost to his ankles. In two years of living beside him, Magik had seen no evidence of gainful employment. "You're dressed up. What's the occasion?"

"Ahh there is this mad dope band playing downtown tonight. Mom is watching the fucking kids so we can hit that shit hard. Gonna be mad sick."

Dani pushed her bike into the garage and almost didn't come out when she saw Billy walk toward Magik.

"Hey brah, I gots a question."

Dani saw Magik walk over to the chain link fence and calculate in his head how much money a taller fence would cost. Billy looked over Magik's shoulder at Dani—he wanted her to leave. Magik threw her the keys and she walked toward the door. Billy whispered but she still heard it. Magik never said yes, but Billy never failed to ask twice a week. "Yo dude, you got any smack?"

"Yeah, no. Sorry we're uh...all tapped out. I even meant to stop at Trader Joes but we totally forgot."

"Aww man it's cool, I was just hopin' and shit. Well thanks anyways. I gots some mad diapers to change." Billy flicked his cigarette into Magik's yard and thumped his fist against his chest before walking to his basement.

Dani pushed open the door and turned around. "Why were they allowed to breed?"

Dawn of the Dead was never meant to look or sound this good. Magik didn't have a TV, just a laptop hooked up to projector that shined onto a large, blank, white wall. The living room was like a minefield filled with speakers. As they settled in for their second movie of the night, some things were becoming clear to Dani. These movies were better than she thought.

The weird, '70s synth music that introduced *Dawn of the Dead* rolled around the surround sound speakers as the movie opened in a hilariously old school TV studio. Dani laughed, and Magik assured her that it was good and that she should keep watching.

"So ,what did you think of *Night?*"

Magik had smiled through the whole movie, sometimes mouthing lines from it. Dani wondered if Magik related to zombies, who managed not to stay dead. Magik loved and lived life to the fullest; he had been in a number of serious accidents. He fell off a cliff in Italy, roller bladed off a pier, and accidentally ate poisonous sushi before he was legal to drink alcohol. The worst happened a week before his third decade started. He had been a banker, big salary, and was two months into a marriage to woman with a Martha Stewart complex. His favorite movie had been *Beaches*.

Maxwell Donnington Junior cruised home in his Lexus after a long day of approving and disapproving loans. At the same time a Border Patrol Agent chased a human smuggler down Interstate 5, followed with a live feed from the KUSI traffic copter. Maxwell was drumming along to Styx on his steering wheel when a sheriff's car spun out of control and slammed into his ass end.

He woke up the next week in a San Diego hospital and had to accept on faith that the nervous looking tight asses sitting by his bed were really his parents. His fair-weather wife had not liked introducing herself again to Max, and liked the idea of the medical bills cutting into her Nordstrom's trips even less. Maxwell didn't remember how to do his job at the bank. He thought "The Wind Beneath My Wings" was annoying and only sought comfort in watching *Star Trek* and reading Robert Heinlein novels.

Like a zombie, Maxwell refused death and reanimated as something different. Thankfully for Dani, he had not turned into a brain-hungry zombie. He had been resurrected a sensitive and caring geek. After settling in divorce court he moved to Portland

and rejected his slave name forever. Dani loved him madly.

"I suppose it's a great movie for its time," Dani said chewing on popcorn. "It's dead people walking and eating people, but what is so deep about it?"

Magik pulled a pillow over his face and groaned. "It was the late sixties. First off, he has a black leading man. In 1968 that was a big fucking deal. Besides, *Night* is a movie for its time, it's about a revolution."

Dani laughed. "I think you're reading too deeply."

"That is the point of a zombie movie, read deeper. The old way is decaying and dying." Magik sighed and grabbed her hand. Dani knew that Magik thought she was a snob sometimes. She was, after all, a snob.

Dani grew up in Ithaca, New York, the child of Cornell professors in English Literature. They met for a family dinner each week night and after dinner shared forty minutes of reading. They cleared the dishes together and discussed the books they read. She was tall at a young age, a gothic beauty who defied the book nerd stereotype. She liked to take charge and read classic literature while rocking Sisters of Mercy and Front Line Assembly on her discman.

A natural-born wordsmith and grammar fascist, Dani spent her first three years after graduate school editing freelance for a few well-known authors, cashing big checks from major publishing houses and shitting massive amounts of income down the black hole of Manhattan. It didn't seem to matter how hard she worked or how big the projects, her closet sized condo on the 62nd floor of her west side high-rise sucked her bank account dry monthly. Dani choose the West Coast, and picked Portland for its reputation as being a progressive, bike-friendly safe haven for freaks.

Dani pointed at the super '70s TV studio. The signature weird keyboard styles of Goblin played on the soundtrack and Dani laughed. "Ok, this is awesome!"

*

By the time the roving biker gang stormed in the mall where the survivors were living in *Dawn of the Dead,* Dani had dozed off several times. Magik had given up on waking her. She cuddled up closer to him. She knew it was a dream, but she found herself back at the Mooch. The hipsters fought to get their hands on the bacon. Tables tipped over, a riot had broken out around her.

"Bacon! Bacon!" A chorus chanted somewhere beyond the immediate reality of her dream.

Dani spun around toward the front door, but this was a dream and the pub spun around with her. Dani stood in place as the pub continued to spin, this time at a snail's pace. Young Portlanders with bike helmets and ironic cowboy boots walked toward her with their arms reaching for a giant pile of bacon in the center of the room. They jumped in the pile and threw the bacon in the air like children playing with fallen leaves. Others ripped and tore at the meat. They drooled and took bites of the pig ass shavings.

Dani felt her popcorn fight to eject, and tried again to back away. The walls spun and Dani felt stuck to her spot as if she was on that spinning G-force ride at a carnival. Dani wanted desperately to scream.

She didn't scream, she didn't jump up, knock the bowl of popcorn on the floor or breath ridiculously heavy like Heather Langenkamp waking up in the original *Nightmare on Elm Street.* Nope, it was a freaky-ass nightmare, but Dani woke up like any other time. She faded into the room. The movie was still rolling, zombies crowded around characters and reached out for them. The people screamed as the zombies tore them in half. Unrealistically large piles of guts and intestines dropped to the mall floor as the zombies fought for delicious morsels of human.

Sleep rolled back over Dani and she saw the pub again. The hipsters suddenly had blue skin and their handlebar mustaches dripped blood. Dani's dream-self screamed, as Magik's curled mustache friend lumbered toward her, his skin rotted off his frame. He groaned as he struggled to speak. His voice sounded like the pumps at the dentist office when they drain your spit. "Don't worry ..."

Dani screamed again.

Mustache's skeletal arms dripped tiny rotted pieces of muscle when he lifted them like a mummy. He continued to talk as green slime poured over dirty and stained teeth. ". . . It's local."

Dani's eyes snapped open. Incredibly silly triumphant music jarred her back to reality. Her eyes took a second to focus but Magik danced in his seat. The lead actor of *Dawn of the Dead* ran with a machine gun toward a lifting helicopter.

"He wants to live!" Magik laughed and Dani buried her head in a pillow.

TEST

1: The director of which of these movies never directed a zombie movie?

    A) *The Lovely Bones*
    B) *A Christmas Story*
    C) *Megiddo: The Omega Code 2*
    D) *Slumdog Millionaire*

2: Magik's most prized zombie possession is:

    A) *A Dawn of the Dead LaserDisc*
    B) *A piece gray latex signed by Tom Savini*
    C) *The Dawn of the Dead targets he uses at the pistol range*
    D) *The Return of the Living Dead soundtrack*

Chapter Three

Magik's black lab, Crom, woke Dani up by licking her face. Dani rolled over. It was ten minutes after six. The dog stared at her. Crom was ready to claim his yard with a healthy dose of urine. Dani had fifty minutes before she would have to bike to work. She looked at Magik, who had a mighty snore going on.

"Okay, Crom." Dani rubbed his head and searched for her jacket. Dani walked through the house and saw her folder from work sitting on the table. The title – *Of Mice and Men with Zombies* -- stared back and reminded her of the day ahead. Great classics of literature deserve to be read, and if it takes the addition of zombies maybe it was a positive thing. Crom didn't care about her job; he simply waited at the door for her. "I'm coming."

The morning air was brisk when she stepped outside. Crom circled the yard looking for the right spot.

"'Sup."

Dani heard the gravelly voice of the woman Magik referred to only as Juggamom. She was built like a linebacker with stringy pink and bright blue hair. She held her cigarette to her face and sucked on it. Dani coughed at the hostile invasion of secondhand smoke.

Juggamom didn't notice as Dani backed up from the fence. "You killahs watched *Dawn of the Dead* last night?"

"Uh," Dani cleared her throat. "Yeah, my first time."

"It's a mad sick movie, yo," Juggamom leaned forward bringing her cigarette closer. She introduced herself but Dani forgot her name by the time she stopped coughing.

"Yeah we like the new *Dawn of the Dead.* It's dark carnival shit, ya' know."

"No. I, uh, don't."

"Dark carnival is like ultimate ride Juggalo-style."

Crom peed through the fence into the Harrison yard. Inwardly Dani approved.

"My oldest boy, he's watched that shit like twenty ass times."

"How old is your boy?"

"He's gonna be seven in three months. Shit, time fucking flies."

Dani looked at her watch. She had plenty of time to get ready, but she didn't want to stand there talking to the Juggamom. "Oh shit, I gotta get ready for work. Crom, let's go."

Crom dug at the end of the fence.

"You got a job, that's cool man. Billy had a job last year. I just fucking watch the little ninjas."

Dani considered for moment that she meant the '80s kid's movie *Little Ninjas* but remembered that Billy called Magik *ninja* like most people called each other dude, or bro. No, Dani concluded the Juggamom was referring to the terrors of the neighborhood—her three children. Dani clapped for Crom, who ran toward her. "Well, parenting is a full-time job."

Juggamom looked confused for a second. "Ahh deep, you mean like Welfare. Where do you, like, work?"

"I am a book editor."

"Awesome, my dude's parents read Newsweek. You work on shit like that?"

Dani opened the door and Crom bolted inside and headed back to bed with Magik. Dani stood there, jealous of the dog. "I should go. I have to leave for work soon."

Dani pushed herself through door and waved. The door shut and she took a deep breath.

"Hey," Juggamom yelled through the door. "We oughta watch dope ass killah zombie movies together. Later."

Dani turned back and gave Juggamom a fake smile. "Sounds nice."

Dani slammed the door and peeked out the window. She watched the Juggamom flick her cigarette onto the official-looking pile on Magik's lawn.

"They don't represent your general zombie fan."

Dani turned around to see a shirtless half asleep Magik stumbling toward his morning coffee. "God, I hope not."

This was really Dani's first full day at the office. Fulci House Press started as a hobby for its founder Brent Hubbard. A full two years before *Pride and Prejudice and Zombies* hit the bestseller list, he had a life changing experience. It came after teaching a brutally disastrous English class at Cleveland High School in Portland, Oregon. It was his second year of teaching English to the inclusion kids; they didn't want to be in school and only seemed interested in reading text message language. He had an idea for the unit on *The Adventures of Huckle Finn*.

Brent remembered being in school. It was a long time before he enjoyed reading, and when he was their age he had been obsessed with zombie movies. Zombie films were the only thing he shared in common with most of his students. Brent couldn't sleep, so he spent all night rewriting *The Adventures of Huckleberry Finn* to include an Old South zombie uprising. His students didn't know the difference, this time they thought the book was cool. Considering the novel was in public domain, it was suggested that he publish the book, to at least sell to his friends.

After *Pride and Prejudice and Zombies* became a bestseller, Brent's little book became a smash hit. Brent knew this was an untapped market—a way to indulge his love of zombie movies, while getting out of the brain sucking void of the high school classroom.

Now Dani was the latest staff member in the 'With Zombie' boom. Six editors worked for Brent. Fulci House had an accountant, a web guy and two dudes who did seemingly important things Dani couldn't put a finger on.

Dani pulled the lunch Magik packed her out of her desk drawer and walked to the break room they shared with one of the insurance companies across the hall. Making friends was never easy for her, so Dani forced herself to go into the room. Her boss, Brent, and one of the unexplained workers sat at a table and offered her a seat. Dani flinched as she smelled the faint smell of BO and campfire behind her. Freddy, one of the other editors, walked in. He looked homeless, but his butt flap with a salvaged 'His Hero is Gone' t-shirt and an anarchy patch screamed punk.

Freddy went straight to the trash can and began digging in it. Brent pushed a chair away from the desk and silently offered Dani a seat. She smiled and sat down.

"Score!" said Freddy as he lifted a half-eaten falafel sandwich out of the trash. Freddy sat down and started to unwrap the scavenged sandwich.

Brent looked at the man across the table from him and laughed. "I knew it."

The man passed a dollar bill over to Brent.

Brent put the bill in his pocket and smiled at Dani. "So, Dani how is day two?"

"Well it's been awhile since I read *Of Mice and Men*."

"Bet you never read it like this before," the other man said. "How do you think I handled the new dialogue?"

Dani stared at him. "You're the author…"

"Not Steinbeck," Brent laughed.

The other man held out his hand. "Luke Spindall."

"Ah yes," Dani smiled. "*Raptor Attack III*, right?"

"They needed a bigger budget for that one."

"My boyfriend is quite fond of the second one, did you write that one?"

"No, just three."

Freddy groaned in delight at his falafel sandwich. Luke shook his head in disbelief.

Brent tapped the table nervously. He had half a Carl's Jr. double cheeseburger left, but his heartburn was already attacking him. "So Luke is just putting the finishing touches on *The Great Zombie Gatsby*. We were thinking, since Salinger is dead now, we need to be ready to roll with *Catcher in Zombie Rye*. What do you think, Dani?"

"Well, if we're not letting the literary bodies grow cold, how about *Cat's Zombie Cradle*?"

Brent and Luke both rubbed their chins. Dani let them think about it as she opened the plastic container Magik packed her. There was a sandwich and something wrapped in a paper towel. Dani opened the sandwich to have a look. Lettuce, tomato and some kind of whitish looking meat. Dani smelled it and instantly flashed back to twenty or so painfully awful Thanksgiving experiences. The family gathered around the golden brown corpse eating bread crumbs out of its hollowed-out ass. The next thing she flashed to was picture of turkeys so fat they could barely stand in the pamphlet she thumbed through at her desk. She resorted to reading *Why Vegan?* when George and Lenny running from zombies became too stupid to bear.

She couldn't eat it. She hoped Magik had wrapped cheese sticks or carrots in the paper towel. Dani pulled gently on the paper but it stuck to something brown holding it. She tugged harder on the paper, pulling it back like a scab off an old cut. Barbecue sauce clung to the paper. Dani realized she was holding a bone broken out of a rib cage and slathered in sugary goop. She was now holding part of a pig's rib cage. She considered the tiny sliver of muscle still attached to the bone and felt nothing but nausea.

Dani put down the container, it felt like a tiny coffin to her now. She put the lid back on it

"Is it moldy? I thought that only happened to us bachelors."

Luke har-har'd to himself and took a bite from his burger. Ketchup dribbled from his lip like blood. His burger was undercooked, red and juicy in the middle. Dani felt queasy, she pushed her chair out from the table and took a big drink of water.

"You okay, Dani?" Brent was still cramping and sat uncomfortably at the table.

"No, I'm fine. I'm just going to get back to work."

"Great idea."

Dani ran back to her desk and threw the lunch container into the trash. Dani took a deep breath and felt a sense of relief. She would rather be hungry than eat that stuff. She turned slightly and almost jumped out of her skin. Freddy stood behind her.

"Oh shit, Freddy. You freaked me out."

Freddy licked his lips slightly. "You done with your lunch?"

Dani nodded, Freddy nodded back.

"Cool," Freddy said as he walked off. Sally, one of the older editors, walked past Freddy holding a bag from McDonald's. As she passed him she put a hand over her face.

Sally sat down at the table across from Dani and opened her McDonald's bag. "I really wish Brent would make him take a shower."

Dani laughed. Sally seemed nice enough, but Dani had a theory that Brent hired her because she looked like a zombie. Her skin was pale, almost gray, and sagged all over her face. She had deep blue circles under her eyes and she walked dragging her left foot all the time.

"How was your lunch?" Sally asked.

"Uh, a life-changing experience." Dani replied.

Sally pulled out her large fries and positioned it. "Really? How?"

"Don't think I'll ever eat meat again."

Sally froze with a Big Mac half-way out of her takeout bag. Sally sighed. "Can you tell me why after lunch? Actually, I don't want to know."

Sally ate a fry and unwrapped her burger, Dani sighed, disbelieving that she was going to eat that thing in front of her.

Sally talked as she chewed on her fries. "Believe me I understand, I'm watching my figure. It took some will power but I'm not getting a sundae anymore. Old habits you know."

The effort of walking down the hallway to the elevator and across the street to the McDonald's had taken Sally's breath away. The trip back was almost too much.

"Don't you wish they delivered?" Sally asked.

"A walk is probably a good thing."

Sally shook her head and opened her mouth wide to take in as much of the Big Mac as she could fit. Dani rolled her chair around to face her computer. She looked at the flyer on her desk; the name of the movie was *Earthlings*. She knew she had plans that night with Magik and they wouldn't be able to make it to the screening. Dani pulled up YouTube and typed in "Earthlings." A trailer and a version cut into ten parts came up.

Dani plugged in her headphones. She had a little time left in her lunch and planned to watch as much as she could. Before she knew it, she was frozen in place watching the film. She wasn't ready for what she saw.

An assembly line of pigs passed by as men in white smocks cut them in half. Dogs were tossed into garbage trucks. A lab tech hit a beagle repeatedly in the face. A primate endured excruciating noises that were piped directly into its brain. A fox, stripped of its fur, lay alive on the killing room floor of the fur farm as it looked at the camera, skinless but aware. An entire harbor filled with the blood of dolphins as men in a boat trapped and shot them. Slaughterhouse workers laughed as they stomped on birds that had fallen off the assembly line. Turkeys ran away flapping their wings as a man coldly walked down a line clubbing one after another.

Dani sat stunned at her desk in tears as the credits rolled—witness to so many haunting and horrific scenes. One thing was for sure, she was never eating meat again.

TEST

1. The following film is a documentary that explores the use of animals as food in our culture?

> A) Flesheaters: Revenge of the Living Dead
> B) Meet your Meat
> C) Night of the Flesh Eaters (AKA Night of the Living Dead)
> D) The Meat Market trilogy

2. Which one of the following titles was not a made for Sci-fi Channel original movie?

> A) Komodo vs. Cobra
> B) Mansquito
> C) Yeti: Curse of the Snow Demon
> D) Man Thing vs. Saber Beast

Chapter Four

They waited in the Volvo outside Dani's apartment building. Crom nervously panted in the back seat. From the moment Magik put him in the car, Crom believed they were going to the park. No park was in sight. Dani walked out to the car and sat a Trader Joe's reusable shopping bag between the seats. Magik looked inside and laughed. It was filled with half-eaten cheeses, a half-empty carton of milk and package of frozen chicken patties.

"What is this?"

"I'm purging, and I want you to take it."

Crom wagged his tail and smelled the bag.

Magik laughed. "What are you, going vegan?"

Dani hadn't said the word yet, but she knew that it was all leading up to this. "Looks like it."

"So, uh yeah, did you know that the first known contraceptive was crocodile dung?"

"First off that's bullshit, second you can't change the subject on me."

Magik mouthed the word shit. Dani sighed.

"I'm going to take it slow. Let's go to New Seasons and I'll get some groceries."

"Big spender," Magik whistled as he put the car in park and moved them closer to the locally owned mini-Whole Foods wannabe. Not quite a health food store, but certainly trying to be.

Dani sat quietly with her arms folded. "Are you making fun of me?"

"No, not at all, it's just . . ." Magik thought carefully about his words. "It's not bullshit, really. Who wants to fuck the dude with croc shit on his package?"

"Goddamn it."

"Well, fuck it. Let's do it together."

"Do what?"

"Veganism." Magik shrugged his shoulders.

Dani had a feeling he was just saying it to make her happy. The fact was it did make her happy. "You'll try."

"My sister is practically vegan. No sweat."

Dani kissed him on the cheek and hoped he was lying to her.

They pushed their basket through the store and picked out lots of new items. When they got to the milk alternatives they stopped in their tracks. Soy, rice, almond and hazelnut milks stared back at them. Vanilla, original and chocolate flavors, sweetened, unsweetened and fortified. So many choices; which ones tasted good, which ones didn't, who knew?

"I thought we went vegan so we wouldn't have so many choices?" Magik said without any irony.

"There were like five different kinds of non-dairy cheese over there?" Dani sounded whiny. A young woman grabbed a carton of almond milk and smiled at them. She was a few years their junior, mildly punk rock with a cute headband holding back her red dyed hair.

"Did you say you were just becoming vegan?"

"Yeah, I guess we are." Magik smiled.

"That's cool, I've been vegan for six years. Don't worry, it will get easier all the time. Oh and about the cheese . . . Teese and Daiya are great, but don't get Vegan Rella, it's gross. Even vegans think so."

The young vegan turned to walk away.

"Wait," Dani put her hand on her shoulder. "Do you have a minute? We could really use your advice."

The young woman thought about it for second. "Yeah sure, have you heard of nutritional yeast?"

They had not heard of it. It was a flaky yellow powder that Diana, their new vegan mentor, said was like gold in a vegan kitchen. Used to make cheese-like sauces and flavor anything from pasta to rice dishes. Diana assured them they would become fans of it on Facebook in no time. She told them which veggie burgers were good, which brands of tofu were runny and which were firm.

"Wow, I think you just saved me months of trial and error."

As they walked through the frozen food aisle, a smell traveled across the store. It was the stench of meat cooking. Magik walked toward the checkout line and followed the smell subconsciously. A woman in rubber gloves smiled at him. He didn't want to admit it, but it smelled good to him.

"Hi, would you like a sample of a delicious SF label pork chop."

Magik looked in the pan and saw the second round of pork and bone sizzling in the hot pan. He looked back at Dani. She was not watching, engaged in conversation with their new friend. He could totally have a bite. One last morsel of meat wasn't going hurt anyone really.

"What does SF label mean?"

The woman smiled. It was then that Magik noticed the USDA community relations name tag on her apron. Her name was Janice; no one under sixty is named Janice. It may not be a stone cold fact, but Magik was pretty sure.

"It means this pork chop was raised by strict Stress-Free animal standards."

Janice handed Magik a flyer, but he wanted the pork, not a flyer. If he didn't sneak it quickly he would miss his window.

"Portland is a progressive community, known for its food awareness. The government thought what better city to premiere Stress-Free meats than Portland."

He skimmed it quickly, but reached for the pork. He felt the heat of the pan, his fingertips just inches from the toothpick stabbing the muscle tissue burning in grease. "What do you mean by stress?"

"Well we understand that many in your community are concerned about the ethical treatment of animals used in the production of food. But you don't have to worry now, not with the Stress-Free label."

Magik stood up straight and looked at the flyer. "Lucky us. So you're going to tell me that they live on a happy farm, sleep on unicorn feathers and get massage therapy up until they get slaughtered. The problem is, lady, they still get slaughtered."

"Yes, they do but it doesn't affect them or the meat at all. Scientists have created a drug that dulls the part of the brain that experiences pain or stress. We don't have to worry about the animals suffering anymore." Janice held out a napkin with a greasy piece of meat.

"Actually I'm vegan."

"Really? For how long?"

"Well, since about ten seconds ago. You talked me into it."

Dani and her new friend Diana walked behind Magik.

"Oh gross," Diana said and lifted her shirt collar up over her nose. "Listen, if you're telling me my meal needs to be injected with drugs not to feel pain I think I'll stick with broccoli."

Janice shook her head. "But Stress-Free label meats have been endorsed by Peter Sangar, the ethics professor and the father of the animal rights movement, not to mention bestselling author Mike Poland."

"Fuck that guy," Diana laughed "He'd eat a turd if it was grass-fed and locally dumped."

"Well in fairness," Magik giggled, "Can you take a dump long distance?"

Janice was not amused. Her face grew red, her blood boiled. "The Stress-Free label is the future of meat. If you don't believe, watch Live at 7 tonight, Poland and Sangar are going to be interviewed. They're going to endorse it, you'll see."

"Honestly, you look a little stressed yourself." Dani said as she tugged on Magik's shirt, pulling him toward checkout. Janice took a deep breath.

"The future of meat! Mark my word you goddamn hippies!"

TEST

1. Mike Poland would eat a human baby if:

    A) It was locally produced

    B) It had not been given growth hormones

    C) A prayer was said thanking the baby for its sacrifice

    D) All of the above

2. Magik decided to be vegan because:

    A) It was easier than having an argument

    B) He was lying and trying to impress Dani

    C) He always felt guilty about eating meat, and just needed a kick in the pants

    D) The author needed him to do it to advance the story

Chapter Five

Magik had vegetarian cooking experience. His sister had been vegetarian since he was young, so it wasn't as if he had never felt a brick of tofu in his hands. Dani, on the other hand, grew up as picky an eater as people come. She was not the world's biggest fan of vegetables, liked pizza, Velveeta Shells and Cheese, and outside of apples she didn't eat much fruit. She probably would have looked a lot less healthy if she wasn't one of those assholes who were born with kind genetics.

"I've eaten tofu before, just never in my own house," Dani said with an embarrassed smile.

Magik raised an eyebrow as he cut open the package. "Tofu is all in how you cook it; it takes on the flavor of the spices."

Dani put on the rice and gave Crom a pat as the dog watched Magik cooking. He was spooning out peanut butter into a pan.

"What is that for?"

"The sauce," Magik playfully snapped a towel at her. "Let me handle this tonight."

Dani laughed and ran into the living room. Crom followed her and picked up a slimy tennis ball. With his eyes, he begged for park, but throwing it into the bedroom would have to do. Dani turned on the TV and threw the ball. She sat on the couch and Crom returned the juicy ball. Dani flipped through the channels and her eyes glossed over. She was two seconds from turning the power off when Magik called out from the kitchen.

"Hey turn on Live at Seven. Channel eight."

Dani flipped the channel as requested. The host Stephanie Strickland stood behind a cooking station with two bald men. Dani rolled her eyes when she recognized the men on the panel and looked back at Magik. He leaned against the kitchen door and wiped his hands. She recognized one of the men from seeing him on Oprah. Infamous locavore activist and author Michael Poland.

"Hey, welcome to the Hot Box. Tonight we have three special guests and a cooking demonstration. First up is Michael Poland, the bestselling author of *It's OK, It's Local*, and *Don't Worry, It's Organic.*"

"Thank you, Stephanie, it is always great to be in Portland," Poland said, as he cracked an egg and dumped the unfertilized ovum into a mixing bowl. He was nerdy-looking in an apron over his expensive suit. He had been a journalist until his book became a bestseller. Now he was a liberal savior treated with Christ-like status at food co-op book signings around the country. It was his book that eased the guilt of millions of consumers who wanted to ignore that there might be anything wrong with the food they were eating every day.

"And joining us again is Portland State Ethics Professor, Peter Sangar, author of *Animal Liberation - OK, OK Welfare.* He is widely considered the father of the modern animal rights movement since his book was published thirty-four years ago."

Sangar nodded at the host. Dani had heard of him, too. He had been an ethics professor at Harvard until he published an article defending what he called "the gentle exploitation of the developmentally disabled." At one time, he had been quite popular in the animal rights movement. Of course, this was around the same time that the American public was obsessed with roller disco and the identity of the person who shot JR.

The camera closed in on the host.

"Everybody loves cute animals, right? Here in Portland we love animals, but we also love to eat bacon, so what to do? A group of scientists have been working on the problem and next week Portland will be ground zero in the new standard of ethical meats and by-products. Tonight we're talking about the premiere of Stress-Free label products, set to hit the streets a week early right here in Portland."

The camera pulled out on a man wearing a chef's hat and aviator sunglasses.

"We have Chef Panic of 11:50 Lounge here and he is going to make scrambled eggs with foie gras hollandaise drizzle."

Michael Poland handed the chef the mixing bowl and he silently acknowledged the camera with his bottom lip and a nod. It was sexy, or at least the chef thought so.

"Who is this dumbass? He is a chef, not Axl Rose." Magik laughed and Dani nodded in agreement.

Chef Panic poured the liquefied ovum into the frying pan and stirred.

The host gestured to Michael Poland. "Mr. Poland, maybe you could explain why you have chosen to endorse the Stress-Free label?"

"Thank you, Stephanie. Well, I have been on the record saying that I think people should eat more plants. If you're going to eat meat, eggs and dairy products, the pain and suffering of farm animals *was* an inherent reality."

"What about small local farms?"

"Right. Generally, I advocate for those types of farms even if you don't really know how the animals are actually treated, because let's face it—feelings of guilt are just not healthy."

The host nodded as Peter Sangar joined in. "We need to reduce the suffering. Now, some have suggested that we should just avoid eating animals."

"Please," Chef Panic scoffed and stirred., "we didn't fight to get to the top of the food chain to eat tofu."

"This drug is a revolution in food production," Poland tried to work his way back into the conversation. "These livestock don't experience stress, anxiety or pain." Poland looked at the camera. "On an average egg farm, even your smaller farms that are considered free range, the stress of constant production affects the flavor of the food. So, not only does the animal suffer, but it doesn't taste like the food our grandparents ate. The thing is with these new drugs the animals live blissfully unaware of their suffering, and it tastes wonderful."

Chef Panic started to drizzle the sauce on a plate of yellow scrambled reproductive tissue. Panic passed the first plate to Poland, the second to Sangar.

"Normally I wouldn't eat eggs, but since it was ethically raised…" Sangar took a small bite and swished it around his mouth.

Poland and the host began to take their first careful bites.

The host stepped forward and smiled at the camera. "This is really good," Strickland said as she swallowed another bite. "So, is this a product that you have to go to a health food store to find?"

"Not at all," Michael Poland smiled with satisfaction. "Thanks to a stimulus package from Congress, all sectors of American agriculture, from beef and chicken to egg and dairy producers, have been engineering livestock with a suppressed anterior cingulate cortex. And within the last few months the drugs have been hitting farms big and small."

"America has been the leader but these products are being introduced globally as we speak," Peter Sangar wiped a tear from his eye. "It is great day for those of us who have fought for so long to reduce animal suffering."

Dani turned the TV off before she threw the remote at it. "Are they fucking kidding?"

"Sadly they are not." Magik appeared with a plate full of tofu and vegetables stir fried with a light peanut sauce. Dani looked up at him and smiled.

Magik crossed his legs and smiled at Dani before taking his first bite. Dani took three quick bites. She closed her eyes and savored the flavor. She felt better about this meal than she had ever felt before. She felt, for the first time, she was eating with a purpose greater than just making poop. She wasn't sure about Magik.

"You didn't want to do this at first?"

"What? Be vegan?" Magik took a bite and used the chewing as excuse to consider his next words carefully. "Ok, I admit I was totally ready to lie, but when that lady was talking about stress and pain. It got me thinking, you know I almost died once in a bowling accident."

"No, I didn't." Dani rubbed his cheek affectionately. "But I suppose if anyone could almost die at a bowling alley it would be you sweetheart."

Magik gave her kiss.

"The point is that, in all the times I've almost died, I've been given lots of pain meds, and I suppose after my accident I was not much more than a nearly dead piece of meat. I understand why you're doing it and I have my reasons. It just made sense."

TEST

1. Peter Sangar was relevant to the animal rights movement when these items were hip and in style:
    A) Glittery Star Wars iron-on shirts
    B) K-Tel 8-track cassette compilations
    C) Station wagons with fake wood panels
    D) All of the above

2. Welfare reforms in animal agriculture have the effect of:
    A) Ending the use of animals as food products

B) Making those who eat non-human animals feel more comfortable

C) Giving animal rights activists a false sense of victory

D) B and C

Chapter Six

At two o'clock in the night of the 13th of June, the Tsar sent for Balashov, and, reading his letter to Napoleon, commanded him to go in person and give the letter to the French Emperor. As he dismissed Balashov, he repeated to him his declaration that he would never make peace as long as a single zombie remained on Russian soil.

Dani spun around in her chair. Her eyes felt like they were bleeding from looking at the text. It had been a mistake to do *Of Mice and Men* so fast. Her speed made her the obvious choice for the epic, *The Zombie War and Peace.* Even in paperback the book was as thick as four bibles. *Hadn't Tolstoy ever heard of a trilogy?*

Sally looked across at her. Gray pallid skin hung off her face, and she had a slight stain from ketchup on the corner of her lip. The napkin she used with her morning hash browns and Egg McMuffin had not been enough. She gasped slowly, not unlike a Romero zombie, between each bite. Every time she ate at the desk, Dani found excuses to go to bathroom or the copy room.

"How is Tolstoy?" Sally asked. She cleared her throat. She looked ready to fall over in her seat.

"Wordy. How is Salinger?"

"I've moved on to Kerouac. *On the Road with Zombies.*"

"Needs a subtitle; *The Deadbeat Generation.*"

Sally nodded, didn't smile or laugh. She never did. Dani turned her

47

chair around. Sally looked like she had aged a decade in the months they'd worked together. In the last month, she was tired and overeating. Her McDonald's trips were becoming compulsive, daily, sometimes involving breakfast. It was harder to look at her day after day.

Dani, on the other hand, felt great. Vegetables. Who knew? When she stayed at Magik's he made them smoothies with leafy greens. She had laughed them off at first. They tasted great. She slept better at night, without the post-frozen-pizza heartburn she used get. She had more energy in the afternoon and started exercising more than once a week.

The only problem was her job. It was nice every other Friday getting a steady paycheck, she felt like a tomb robber going through these great works of literature and making sure that Luke's grammar matched the source when he added hordes of brain-hungry zombies. It frustrated her, but she rode her bike in every day, locked up at the bike rack and kept her head down until time to leave.

Dani didn't socialize with her co-workers. She learned about them from her desk, where she took her breaks and ate her lunch everyday. Her interactions were mostly with Sally, who she learned had the sense of humor of a war tribunal. Dani's sense of humor and Sally's were like oil and water, an uncomfortable mix that never merged.

The whole office was a hodgepodge of different Portland hipster genres, all of whom rode their bikes as fashion accessories and thought that getting drunk in Santa outfits at SantaCon was enough to keep Portland weird. Brent was the boss but spent most of the day reading every *with Zombies* page that went across his desk. Today, he was talking to a friend all morning in his office. Dani had not caught his name; everyone just called him Bru-Dawg.

Dani could see Bru-Dawg, jean jacket with a punk patch on it, blond hair, glasses and belt made of bullet shells. Bru-Dawg laughed every once in a while, shaking the walls. Even through the walls his deep laughter was impressive in its bass.

Trish, who worked at the front desk, was a former college cheerleader and current tattooed hipster. Rumors flew around the office that she stripped on weekends at a club for guys with tattoo fetishes. Several of the editors at Fulci House were old college friends of Brent's from Indiana. Sally grew up in Ashland, Oregon, a few hours south, but for whatever reason every third person she met in Portland was from Indiana and if they were in the right age range they all seemed to have gone to college with or hung out with her boss.

The door to the office opened and it was Rich from the insurance agency across the hall. Rich was a Southeast Portland native who was going bald by the time he hit thirty. As duty demanded, he shaved his head hairless, sans the soul patch under his lip. Rich had a daily excuse for coming into the office and, while he was friendly to everyone, it was as obvious as the stupid hair on his chin that he was crushing on their receptionist.

"Hey Trish, would you like to taste some caramel glazed bacon?" Rich dipped his bowl so she could get a handful. The rest office all leaned out of their cubicles and looked toward the front desk.

Trish took a bite and smiled at him. "Did you bring those just for me?"

Rich's bald head got red with embarrassment. Dani had watched this sickening game for a month now. Rich didn't want to come on too strong, so whatever nice thing he offered Trish he ended up offering to the whole office. He once took everyone out for a Friday happy hour, which set him back.

"Caramel glazed bacon. Stress-Free label, anybody want to try?"

One by one the entire office gathered. Brent and his friend came out last. Her co-workers bit into the bacon and one after another complimented Rich on his creative use of ass shavings.

"Gross dude," Bru-Dawg said with a voice unnaturally deep for his slender build.

"No kidding." Dani turned back to her computer. One of the

editors, Keith, walked up her desk. He dripped caramel on his path.

"This bacon is baddass, you going to get some?"

"Ahhh no thanks, I'm vegan." Bru-Dawg said. Dani stopped and looked up. She had avoided the topic at work. She didn't want to catch shit from her coworkers. Diana, her vegan mentor, had told her horror stories of being a vegan in the workplace. The people who start a conversation by telling them they wish they could eat like you but then babble endlessly about how they could never live without cheese. The co-worker who tries to challenge you with insane hypotheticals trying to get you to say you would eat meat if you had to. And worst of all the dreaded ex-vegan.

Brent's friend didn't seem to mind telling them he was vegan. Dani was an outspoken person, a natural smart ass. Suddenly she felt like a wimp. If this dude could tell everyone he was vegan, well damn it, so could Dani.

"Yeah no thanks I'm vegan too." Simple, It's done and the earth didn't end. Luke the author turned around when she said it.

"Bullshit, your first day I saw you eating ribs."

Dani sighed and took a deep breath. "I never ate it. It was after that anyways."

Luke laughed.

"Fuck that. Eat some bacon. It's like fucking candy dude."

Dani looked over Luke's shoulder and saw the other vegan had walked back into Brent's office. Dani wanted to ask the author of *Raptor Attack III* to back the fuck off. She just folded her arms. Luke stepped closer. Freddy, the hobo-looking punk rock editor, walked up with him.

"So why don't you eat meat?" asked Luke.

"I was vegan in college," said Freddy. *The dreaded ex-vegan.* He was dreaded in more than one way. He had nappy dreadlocks and punk patches sewn over his butt patch. He was the most punk rock person in the office. So punk rock he would answer Luke's question, the question he had asked Dani. Freddy had train hopped here from

Indiana and asked Brent for a job a few weeks back. Despite the fact that he smelled like a campfire and dumpster sludge the guy could edit.

Ex-vegans were dreaded because they talk down to people who are currently vegan like they are two-year-olds who just need to grow up and eat a hamburger like everyone else. This was Dani's first experience with the dreaded ex-vegan. Retreat was her best option.

"You know, I don't feel comfortable talking about this."

"Yeah I understand, it can really seem like you're making a difference." Freddy patted Dani's hand. She fantasized about Freddy combusting, but smiled. Inside she had started a silent mantra of *Please go away.*

"Wait, I have a serious question." Luke turned a chair around and rolled up to Dani's desk. "So let's say you're on a desert island and there is a cow. You'd eat it right?"

"I wish I could be vegan," Sally said and sucked drool back in before it slipped out of the right side of her mouth. "I just don't know what I would do without french fries."

"Well, about the island," said Freddy, never giving Dani a chance to tell Sally potatoes are a vegetable. "You have to survive. So, I'm sure Dani would eat the cow."

"Excuse me, but no, I would not eat the cow."

"It's just a cow and you need to survive," Luke added.

"Listen brainiacs, what is the cow eating?"

Luke and Freddy looked at each other. Freddy cleared his throat.

"That's not the point of the question."

"Ah ha!" Dani pointed at him. "The point of the question is stupid. The cow has to eat vegetation. Well, so would I, but that is not the bigger issue."

"What's that?" asked Sally.

"The bigger issue is that I would not be on a desert fucking island." Dani gave them as angry a face as she could but Luke and Freddy still stood there.

"So why do you eat meat Freddy?" Luke asked.

"Actually guys, I'm editing *War and Peace,* so could you maybe have this discussion at one of your desks. Luke, don't you have *Raptor Attack IV* to write or something?"

"Yeah man," Freddy pulled up a chair and sat down next to Dani. "I agree factory farms are messed up, no doubt. The problem is agriculture itself."

Freddy didn't seem to understand you are supposed to listen to other people in a conversation. Dani could tell he wasn't going to leave. She was cornered at her desk. The only answer, attack.

"So how the fuck are we supposed eat if we don't grow food?"

"I'm a primitivist," Freddy said, just before his cell phone beeped. Dani stared in amazement as he got out his Blackberry and started typing a text message.

"So is there an app to help you go spear hunting?" Dani rolled her eyes.

Freddy snapped his phone shut. "You know how much land is destroyed growing soybeans? The problem is not inherent to meat."

"I disagree. Most of those soybeans are fed to cows, Freddy. Sixteen pounds of grain for every pound of beef, dude. If your fucking problem is with agriculture there would be a hell of lot less of it if we were growing food for us, not pigs and cows."

"Look Dani, agriculture is destroying the planet," said Freddy.

"Wild lands are almost gone. You're not going to feed six billion people with a bow and arrow and a Ted Nugent complex, it's too goddamn late. We better find some more gentle form of agriculture or you're going to have a lot of hungry hunters."

"Look, I only eat food waste. So much food gets thrown away in this country," said Freddy.

"Right, so you're a parasite who depends on others making bad choices."

Freddy was about to disagree when Keith pulled up a chair. "Me, I love steak."

Dani sighed. Keith took no cue.

"My question for you fucking vegans is this. What do you do with the fucking cows if you don't eat them? It's simple math dude, those bovine fuckers will take over in like ten years."

Dani daydreamed about shooting Keith dead. Right there in the office, out of her misery. The question was so stupid it made her brain hurt.

A whistle carried across the room. Brent stood by his office door. "Can I see everybody for a minute?"

The whole office crew assembled outside Brent's door. Trish waved bye at Rich who almost followed her into the meeting. Bru-Dawg rolled out a TV and VCR.

"Bring a chair with you."

Dani looked at Sally. "What is this?"

"Team building exercise. We haven't done one in a while."

Dani rolled up her chair.

"Ok, folks it's been a while since Bru-Dawg showed us a movie."

Dani looked at Luke as he sat next to her.

"Yeah Bru-Dawg is a friend of ours from . . ."

"Indiana right?"

"Yeah, he is a librarian and zombie film expert."

"IU gives degrees in that?"

Brent stepped forward. "Last year we watched some of the B-movie Italian zombie films, and it's important to me as authors and editors here at Fulci House that you have an understanding of the roots of the wider genre."

Bru-Dawg stepped forward. "So the movie we're going to watch today is kind of a Z-grade Italian film called *Burial Ground* by zombie auteur Andrea Bianchi.

Dani looked around. Freddy took his shoes off, an act followed by nervous coughing and more than one shirt collar gas mask pulled over office noses. Trish shook a bag of microwave popcorn. Sally had fallen asleep.

Dani leaned over to Luke. "We're just going to watch a movie?"

Brent shushed them. "Go ahead, Bru."

"Yeah, so, some things to look out for are the zombies working together and use of tools. Personally, and this not zombie-related, but my favorite part is the ten-year-old kid. The director decided to cast what appears to be a thirty-year-old man with some kind of dwarf condition, and then had him dubbed by a guy doing some kind of falsetto. Pretty creepy."

Brent pushed play and the old fuzzy VHS played. Bru-Dawg adjusted the tracking. "Really, the older the tape, the better the movie looks."

When the lights went out, Dani rolled her chair quietly back to her desk. The movie was out of sight but she could hear the painfully bad dubbing. The office erupted in laughter several times. Brent came around the corner a half-hour later. Dani was plugging away at the editing but still felt like she had been busted.

"What are you doing?"

"Working."

"What do zombies eat?"

Dani sighed. "Uh brains."

Brent shook his head, disgusted. "Sometimes, but most zombies will eat any flesh they can get their hands on. *Return of Living Dead* can be blamed for that misconception."

"Why only humans, Brent?"

"Excuse me?"

"Well, I've been thinking. Humans eat flesh all the time, they just eat animal flesh. Why don't zombies do that?"

Brent thought about it. "You know Bru-Dawg and I were college roommates. In one year I think we watched every zombie movie known to the human race. I don't think that has ever been explained."

Dani held out her hands and shrugged.

"You know Dani, some people would kill to have a job where they were paid to watch bad Italian rip-off movies."

Dani didn't protest, just rolled her chair back to sit in front of the movie. This movie was the final straw. She hated zombies. She had had enough of zombies. The word itself drove her crazy. Each time she read it, she felt like it was taking a bit of her soul. Dani lowered herself in her chair and got out her cell phone. She sent a text message to Magik.

Drink after work?

TEST

1. Italians made several low budget rip-offs of films in the following genres:

 A) Zombie movies
 B) Westerns
 C) 'Nam vet/ one-man army movies
 D) All of the above

2. The only reason a cow would be on a desert island would be:

 A) Some idiot human put him/her there
 B) To prove without a shadow of doubt that humans being vegetarian is impossible
 C) To film an episode of Lost
 D) To get away from humans

Chapter Seven

Magik walked into the office just as the end credits of *Burial Ground* mercifully ended Dani's mandatory employment torture session.

Magik squinted at the screen and pointed like a tween who got a surprise glimpse of a Jonas brother. "*Burial Ground!*"

Dani slumped in the chair and wished she had a hat to pull over her face.

Brent clapped his hands twice. "Tomorrow, we'll start to roll out the spring line. I want some ideas for more classics with zombie novels for the fall."

Luke lumbered away and nodded as Freddy explained how he thought the zombies in *For Whom the Bell Tolls* should side with the fascists. Sally and the editor, Keith, discussed *The Last of the Zombified Mohicans.*

Magik nodded in approval and sat down next to Dani. "How can you not love working here?"

"Well," Dani whispered. "I hate zombies for one thing, and for another thing, Luke asked me this totally dumbass question."

"It wasn't the one about the desert island and the cow was it?"

Dani looked surprised. Magik didn't have co-workers and almost never left the house. "Who asked you that?"

"Pizza guy."

Dani stood up. She already knew where she wanted to go. The Someday Lounge, just a few blocks away had an amazing barbecue tempeh wrap. She pulled Magik toward her cubicle. "Let's go to Someday."

"Bad idea, tonight is the 'Dress Like a Robot' industrial dance."

Dani sighed, knowing that Magik was one step from asking her to go to Dante's. It was her least favorite bar. Magik always wanted to go there. She didn't even have her bag collected and was basically too exhausted to argue.

"Dante's?"

Dani faked a smile. "Why not."

Zombies were why not. It was the third annual Dante's Zombie Prom. Hipsters in formal tuxes and dresses splattered in blood and their faces made up to look like the living dead. Magik laughed as they stood by the bouncer at the front door. Dani just stared inside in disgust. Dressing like a zombie, pretending to be a zombie, was now a hip and cool activity.

"Five dollar cover, six if you're not dressed like a zombie."

Dani heard someone moan before a couple dragged their feet up to the door. The zombie prom date slowly lifted a rigor-stiff arm up with a five dollar bill for the bouncer.

"Thank you," the bouncer said and stamped his hand.

"Brains," groaned the zombie as he shuffled past.

Dani looked at Magik. "They only do that in one movie."

"Yeah," Magik laughed. "But *Return of Living Dead* is an important one."

A couple walked past in silver robot costumes, one dressed like Twiki from *Buck Rogers,* the other like Robbie the Robot from *Lost in Space*. A man dressed in torn zombie clothes and a fake ripped-out eyeball hanging off his face blew cigarette smoke at Dani (who brushed it away and coughed) as he watched the robots pass.

"What dorks," the hipster zombie said and flicked his cigarette into the street. The hipster zombie showed his hand stamp and went back inside.

"Tube?" Magik asked, knowing Dani would not go to the Zombie Prom.

They went to another bar called the Tube. After they ate three vegan 'ham' and 'cheeze' sandwiches and a big salad, Dani felt better. She managed to go a half-hour without thinking about zombies. Dani watched as a woman came back from having a cigarette to the bar. She wore knee-high leather boots, fishnet stocking and a fur coat. Magik didn't whistle as most men would, he hissed.

Dani didn't hear him and smacked his knee. Magik turned and knew Dani believed he was staring at this woman. Dani's eyes came close to striking him dead, silently communicating *don't look at that fur hag.*

Magik cleared his throat. "Did you know Isaac Asimov is the only author to have a book in every Dewey Decimal category?"

Dani shook her head. "You were looking at her."

Magik looked at Dani. Her bobbed hair framed her perfect face. Her smile and bright teeth shined through the dark bar. He really did love her.

Magik laughed. He grabbed her hand. "Actually, I was grossed out by the coat."

Dani believed him, but still she looked emotionally shaky. Like tears were floating near the surface.

"What's wrong?"

"That's just it," Dani pushed the remains of her sandwich across the table. "I feel great. Better than ever, but it's Sally at work. She looks awful."

"Like sick?"

"It's hard to look at. More like. . . I don't know, dead."

Magik smiled with a shit eating grin.

"Don't say it," Dani rolled her eyes.

"Like a . . ."

"Don't say it!" Dani put her hand up.

"A zombie!"

"Stop. Please," Dani looked up at the ceiling.

"They're coming to get you, Dani," Magik put his arms out like a mummy. Dani waved at him like she was brushing away smoke.

"I'm serious, something is wrong with her."

Magik settled down when a scream sounded across the bar. The music stopped. They turned to see the woman in the fur coat pinned against the bar. An older looking man was standing over her. She screamed a second time as the bartender ran around the bar and pulled the old man off of her. The old balding man tried to bite her. The woman at the bar cried and screamed before moving down the bar.

"Professor Sangar, stop!" the bartender yelled. Dani looked at the old man fighting in the bartender's grip. Wild gray hair, glasses, and a blood stained sweater. The old man continued to struggle in his grip. Dani looked at the crazed eyes and almost missed it. The ethics professor she had seen on the TV!

Magik looked at Dani. The furred woman hugged herself as she checked the coat for damage.

"Fuck!" the woman screamed. "It's vintage, stupid fucking vegans!"

The bartender pushed the professor away from her. The professor groaned and dribbled chunks of flesh on his sweater.

Friends of the woman in the fur coat ran to help her. She screamed again. "First they throw paint now this!"

Dani looked at Magik. "Let's get out of here."

They stood up to leave, and got a better look at the professor. His skin was a light tinge of blue. Dani gasped when she saw his bloodshot eyes. Despite the calls for him to sit down, he struggled in the bartender's grip and even bit at him. Dani pointed at the scene.

"Are you seeing this?"

"Yeah, that dude looks pretty wasted."

Dani and Magik ran for the door. Once out on the street they put on their bike helmets and walked toward their bikes. The city block around Dante's was blocked off. Traffic and buses stopped, and a crowd gathered. Several dozen police cars had piled up in front of the club. Zombie-dressed hipsters lined up behind the police tape.

Magik tapped on the shoulder of one of the zombies.

"What happened?"

"One of the zombies just fucking bit one of the robots."

Dani laughed. "I knew it," Dani giggled. "This scene just isn't big enough for robots and zombies."

"This isn't funny, man," another zombie spoke up. "They just tasered my buddy, Ray."

Magik looked past the spinning red lights and saw a man dressed in torn zombie clothes and who had about six different strings of taser attached to his body. He shook violently, like a carrot sticking out of a juicer, before he hit the pavement. Cops shouted. His friends cried out and the zombie groaned.

"I didn't even know Ray was coming to Zombie Prom," said Ray's friend as he shook his head in disbelief.

Ray stood up awkwardly and marched forward.

"On the ground or we will open fire!"

Magik watched, stunned. Dani hit his shoulder. She took a step in the direction of their bikes. Magik didn't move. Dani sighed.

"Come on let's go."

Magik was stunned that she was not freaked out by the scene in front of them. He pointed at Ray, who ripped away the taser lines like Godzilla through Tokyo power lines.

"Don't you think they are overdoing it?" Dani dug through her bag looking for her bike lock keys. "This zombie act, just a little overboard."

The police speaker on top of the car told Ray to get on the ground and several weapons clicked and popped. Ray stopped and cocked his head. A scream carried out of the bar as several other zombies squeezed through the door like a crowning turd and burst into the street.

"See, that's just ridiculous," Dani shook her head and pulled on Magik's arm. They moved away down the street, behind them choruses of unearthly gravelly groans called out to the night.

"No way Dani! Those cops are real."

"Give me a break," Dani kept walking. "It's like that nimrod who organized the giant *Thriller* dance or the ride-the-train-in-underwear day. A bunch of hipsters who want to keep Portland weird."

Magik pointed back at the scene. A second later, gunshots boomed down the street. Magik jumped to Dani and held on to her. Screams followed and the hipsters dressed like robots and zombies suddenly ran toward them as if the doors had opened at Wal-Mart on Black Friday. Dani pushed Magik out of the way.

Some of the people laughed, a few cried, and few screamed bloody murder. Just when the echo of the gunshots had convinced Dani this had to be real, a person rolled by in a functional black Captain Pike wheelchair from the original Star Trek.

Dani laughed and unlocked her bike. Magik stared back at the scene. Another gun shot rang and was followed by screams and a voice over the police loud speaker. "Zombies! Stand down. This is an order."

Magik scratched his long Nordic blond hair. "Ok, that has to be a joke."

TEST

1. Good vegan food options at downtown Portland bars include:
    A) Tube 'Ham and Cheeze' Sandwiches
    B) Portland Teese Steak at Someday Lounge
    C) Vegan pizza at Fifteen
    D) All of the above

2. *It is a good idea to have a bulletproof vest in Portland if you:*
   A) Work security at a Trailblazer game
   B) Work as a Principle of a high school
   C) Drive a public bus
   D) Surrender yourself to the police

Chapter Eight

"Yo dawg, there's some psychopathic shit goin' on downtown. Can you like watch our kids and shit?"

Magik and Dani still had their bike helmets on. Billy Harrison fought for breath after running the five-foot length of his yard. Dani looked behind Billy and saw the elder Harrisons on the couch watching *Wheel of Fortune*. Magik had never watched children, let alone three children raised by his barely functioning Juggalo neighbors. Dani stared at Magik like a deer caught in the headlights of an eighteen-wheeler.

"I don't know Billy, can't your parents help you out with that?"

Billy frowned. He looked down at his Twizted hockey jersey stained with three days worth of TV dinners. "Fuck, man I heard there was like zombies and fucking robots fighting. I mean, like how often do you get to see that crazy-ass shit."

Dani held in laughter. As heartbreaking as this display was, Crom was in the window wagging his tail. He wanted out in the yard to water the grass. Billy lit a cigarette.

"Gee, I'm sorry Billy." Magik coughed at the smoke. "Far be it from me to deny you any crazy-ass shit, but we need to walk the dog and we have an early day . . ."

"Fuck, man," Billy flicked the smoke into Magik's yard and walked back to his basement. "See if I ever watch your lame-ass kids."

Dani was amazed he didn't ask for smack. Billy opened the door, was half way through when he stopped. Dani could almost see the light bulb singeing his dyed-green hair. Billy turned around.

"Yo, y'all don't happen to have any smack?"

Magik shook his head.

"You know, I knew I was forgetting something."

Dani laughed this time. Magik tightened his lips and managed to get through the door without cracking up. Crom barked at them as they laughed. Dani grabbed Crom's leash and ran with him back out the door. Magik stayed behind to make tea.

Crom ran across the yard to his favorite spot on the Harrison's chain link fence. Dani walked through the yard to find the growing pile of cigarettes that Billy and the Juggamom had thrown into Magik's yard. One cigarette still smoked on the top. The pile was too high to step on. Dani just moved away from it.

Crom circled the edge of the yard and sniffed. Dani heard the familiar sound of the Harrison's basement door opening followed by the screams of little voices. The Juggamom followed her three slightly obese children into the yard and lit a cigarette. Dani thought about offering her the one still burning in the yard.

"Alright, I guess we'll play zombie because our pussy ass neighbor won't watch you," Juggamom practically yelled.

Dani squeezed the leash out of frustration and Crom looked back at her surprised. She should have been annoyed with the not-so-passive-aggressive statement. That didn't bother her. It was watching the Jugga-kids groan and stumble around the yard like zombies.

Dani whistled and led Crom down the sidewalk. As they walked away, she heard a tiny three-year-old make spittle flinging machine gun noises.

"Die you faggot-ass zombie fucks," the little boy called out.

Dani picked up the pace, to get away quickly. Crom was happy to run. Still the day boiled over and she couldn't hold it in. "Fuck!"

Enough with the goddamn zombies! Zombie team building exercises at work, zombie proms and drunk ethics professors who think they are zombies were enough. Why the fuck does everyone suddenly think a rotting stinky-ass corpse that walks is so cool and hip? What is so damn rad about eating brains? What is cool about rotting standing up?

Crom circled the block leading Dani to the same spots he always did. They stopped at a wooden fence. Crom liked to smell this post. He sniffed it over and over refusing to move on for several minutes. Dani let out a deep breath and watched it rise in the cool air. When the breath cleared, Dani jumped. A man walked in the street toward them.

His large frame was lit from behind by a street light. His face was in shadow, and his leg appeared to be twisted at an awkward angle.

"Hello," Dani smiled but stopped short of saying good evening.

The man walked toward her and groaned. His slow march in her direction continued. Dani shook Crom's leash, but the dog sniffed the fence, entranced by the ghostly smell of fifteen other dogs whose urine varnished this fence daily.

"Crom, let's go."

The dog may have heard Dani but didn't react; his nose scanned the fence surface. The man walked closer and his face caught the light from the far street lamp. His eyes were wide open and looked yellow. His head tilted to the side and red drool drained out of his mouth. Dani yanked a little harder on the leash. Crom looked at her but only squeezed closer to the fence and crawled into the bush against it.

The man stepped closer. He didn't look like a man. Dani knew what he looked like but the goddamn irony of it pissed her off.

"Can you help me?" The man struggled with his words.

Dani relaxed bit and then her face grew red with embarrassment. She had entertained for a moment that this homeless guy was actually a zombie. Dani wiped her forehead and thought about calling in sick to work. She must need a day off to not think about zombies.

Bones creaked and snapped as the old guy lifted an arm and pointed at her. "Do you know where I could find a Carl's Jr.?"

"No, sorry man I don't eat that kinda stuff."

"Really," the man said and groaned. "You're some kind of vegetarian?"

Crom stepped out and walked to the length of the leash. Dani held him in place. "Yeah, I'm a vegan."

The man laughed. "You don't look sick."

"No, I feel great."

The man took a painful step. He moved past her at a pace only worms could envy. "Figures. It has to be the goddamn meat."

Dani suddenly felt very sorry for the man. Crom pulled at the leash going in the opposite direction. "Being vegetarian is pretty easy sir," Dani felt Crom's less-than-gentle tug.

The man waved back at her but kept walking.

TEST

1. That man was:

    A) Homeless

    B) A zombie

    C) Not quite a zombie

    D) In need of a good stretching routine

2. The Harrisons did not want to babysit their grandkids because the last time they did:

    A) The five-year-old did not like to watch grandpa's "lame-ass shit on TV"

    B) The three-year-old put a cat turd in grandpa's denture holder

C) The five-year-old shot twelve pieces of fine china with a sling shot
D) All of the above

Chapter Nine

Dani typed at her desk. She had not looked at any work since she got to the office that morning. Actually doing what she was supposed to do meant cracking open her massive, bible-thick copy of *Zombie War and Peace.* She wanted nothing to do with that. Instead she spent the first hour and a half of her work day looking up information about Juggalos, the underground music scene Magik's neighbors were a part of. She closed her web browser quickly when Keith pulled up a rolling chair. He rolled up to Dani's desk. She wanted to run. These talks happened now multiple times each day.

"Protein? Where do you get your protein?"

"Food," Dani tried to say the word with as much nastiness as she could.

"You need at least something like fish right?"

"No, really I don't."

Keith shook his head like a bobble toy. He really thought he had her beat in this debate he tried everyday to start with her. He pointed and laughed. It was like there was an angel on her shoulder telling her to explain calmly that there are plenty of sources of protein in a vegan diet. The devil on her other shoulder just wanted her to tell Keith he was a little fucker and to get out of her face.

"You're gonna get sick."

Dani looked over Keith's shoulder at his desk. He had a wastebasket pulled out by his chair for easy barfing. His skin looked pale and he had bags under his eyes. The devil on her shoulder felt emboldened. Dani cleared her throat. "Is that your barf bucket, Keith?"

"Yeah, just a little under the weather."

"As much as I love these little talks of ours, I get plenty of protein. It doesn't hurt the cows if you don't milk them. Soy bean farming sucks but most of it is fed to cattle. And if we didn't breed animals for food, they wouldn't exist, so not eating them will not cause a cow uprising. So please go back to your desk, and don't ever come back over unless you have a zombie editing question. OK?"

Keith muttered, "bitch", or at least he mouthed the words as he got up. At almost the same time, Brent walked past her desk on the way to his office.

"Hey, Brent."

Dani chased her boss down in the hallway. She had psyched herself up all night to talk to him.

"Walk with me."

Dani smiled and kept her pace following him toward his office. "So I realize this would be a departure, but I thought of a book that I think we should do. Wide commercial appeal."

Dani followed Brent into his office and found Bru-Dawg sitting at his desk with a stack of DVDs.

"Dani here has an idea for new zombie book."

Dani looked at both of them and swallowed. Brent sat in front of his framed subway style *Zombie* poster that said *We are going to eat you,* in Italian. He leaned back in his chair. He didn't look healthy, had bags under his eyes and stretched uncomfortably in his chair.

This will make him feel better, Dani thought. "Picture this," Dani cleared her throat, "*Anna Karenina, Vampire Hunter.*"

Bru-Dawg groaned. Brent shook his head.

Dani panicked. They were not into it. She put up her finger. "And, *Beowerewolf.*"

Bru-Dawg almost fell out of his chair. Brent slapped his hand on his table. His laughter turned to coughing.

"Lame," Bru-Dawg giggled.

Brent's cough finally cleared. "Dani, I know you're new here and have missed several of the team building sessions with Bru-Dawg."

Bru-Dawg put his thumb up.

"This is Fulci House Press." Brent rocked in his chair. "Bru, what was Lucio Fulci famous for?"

"Killer zombie movies."

"That's right. We're on a mission to get mindless followers who would never read a classic of literature to think of Tolstoy or Hemingway as killer books. In college we turned to Fulci movies to clean out our brains after class. Fulci inspired me to do this. "

Dani nodded, pretending to understand. To take this lecture to heart. Brent had done more than knock the wind out of her sails, he tipped over the boat. One more try. "I just think it might be cool if we expanded. You know, branch out."

Bru-Dawg rubbed his chin. "You know dude, she may have a point." Bru-Dawg put down his stack of DVDs. "Fulci did more than zombie movies."

"Yeah," Brent smiled. "Spaghetti Westerns, and the Texas Gladiator movie."

"No dude, that futuristic Texas gladiator movie was another Italian."

"Joe D'Amato!" they said together.

Brent went back to his bookshelf filled with DVDs. Many were imports of uncut versions of B-movies, not popular enough outside of Japan to be sold anywhere else. Brent laid a DVD on his desk. The cover had a man with mohawk and battleaxe riding in a dune buggy.

"Classics of American literature with gangs of punk rock gladiators." Brent said and leaned back in his chair.

"Killer dude," Bru-Dawg agreed.

Dani couldn't believe her ears. Brent pushed the DVD toward Dani.

"You should watch this movie, it's really bad."

Dani looked at the DVD in her hand. Her little chat with the boss didn't exactly go as planned. Luke walked past her and looked down at the DVD.

"Eww, yikes, that movie is total shit."

Luke walked on. Dani watched as he crossed the office. Luke dragged his leg slightly, like it was chained to a heavy weight. Dani walked to her desk and saw an almost-green-looking Keith cough at his desk, he had a trash can pulled up to his office chair for emergency hurling.

Dani sat down and rolled her chair around to face Sally. The woman sat at her desk, her head rocking back and forth. Her eyes were bright yellow, her skin was wrinkled and purple, her hair was stiff and buffed out like she was in an '80s hair metal band.

Dani looked around. The office moved on, keyboard patter, phones ringing, coffee being poured. No one seemed to notice Sally looking ill at her desk.

"Sally, uh, are you alright?"

The response was delayed. At first, Sally didn't look as if she understood or even heard Dani. Her mouth opened with a series creaks that sounded like a roller coaster climbing. "Ahhhhh."

Dani looked around. Sally's breakfast sat in a bag from McDonalds. Dani grabbed it off the desk.

Sally opened her mouth. "Ahhhhh."

Dani unrolled the bag and the smell of sausage escaped. She pulled out a wrapped sandwich, with a Stress-Free label on the yellow wrapper. Both the eggs and the sausage were Stress-Free label products. Dani threw it back in the bag.

"Sally I told you this stuff was bad for you."

"Ahhhhh."

"You can't eat this shit everyday."

"Ahhhh."

71

"I don't wanna be preachy. You understand, right?"

"Ahhhhh."

Dani put the bag back down on the table. Sally didn't look at it hungrily, she looked at Dani's arm. Sally leaned over and reached for Dani. Dani pulled her arm back and Sally fell with her face against the desk.

"Sally!"

"Ahhhh," Sally said muffled by the desk.

Dani stood up and walked back to Brent's office. Dani knocked on the door, but opened it quickly. Bru-Dawg pointed at a DVD— *Nightmare City*.

"Now, this film represents a similar progression in the Italian zombie canon. Here, the undead can actually run and fire machine guns, as well as use blades. This could also be classified as a political zombie film, because the outbreak is caused by an environmental catastrophe. I only wish there were a midget kid." Bru-Dawg kept talking as Dani walked up to Brent's desk.

"Sally is a fucking zombie."

"Woah," Bru-Dawg said in his best *Point Break* imitation. Brent didn't look healthy either, but not as purple as Sally.

"A zombie here at the office?"

"Well, that or she is sick. You know what? Keith is coughing, and frankly you look a little under the weather yourself."

Brent looked at Bru-Dawg, Bru nodded in agreement.

"You do have a Roger toward the end of *Dawn of the Dead* thing going on," said Bru-Dawg before they both laughed.

Dani pointed back at her desk. "Just have a look."

Brent and Bru walked across the office toward Sally. She had sat back up and rocked again in her seat. Sally stared off into the distance. Brent leaned in front of Sally and snapped his fingers. She didn't react. Her eyes were comically wide open and Sally never blinked. Brent looked back at Dani and Bru.

"Dude, you know what Napalm Death says?" Bru cupped his

hands like he was holding a microphone and did a death metal growl. "DEAD!"

Brent stepped back and looked at Dani. "No, she's sitting up at her desk." Brent leaned in, put his hand on her shoulder and cleared his throat. "Sally, you don't look so hot today, and I think it might be better if you, I don't know, maybe go home and get some rest."

Sally's head twisted toward Brent with a creak and snap.

"Ahhhhh."

Brent took a step back. "Yeah, OK."

Luke walked up behind them ,stumbling. He had trouble walking, like he was super drunk.

"Bosssss," Luke spoke in voice just above a growl. "I think I need to go home."

Brent looked around, everyone but Dani and Bru stumbled or were keeled over holding their stomachs. "Yeah let's all get the fuck out of here."

It was like a signal starting a race. Everyone gathered their belongings and moved as fast as they could. Dani grabbed her lunch and her purse. She saw Bru-Dawg leaving quickly with a stack of DVDs under his arm.

"Hey Bru, you got a second."

"Fuck no. I don't want to get sick."

Dani grabbed his arm. "You look fine."

"I'd rather stay that way."

"Have you noticed people acting strange?"

"It's Portland."

Dani laughed. Keith groaned and stumbled past them out the door.

"Let me ask you Bru-Dawg, as an expert, what would you do in a zombie apocalypse?"

"Blaze of glory dude, blaze of glory."

TEST

1. At this point Sally should:
 A) Eat her breakfast
 B) Get some rest
 C) Have a drink
 D) Be shot in the head immediately

2. In case of a zombie outbreak, the office policy is:
 A) Find a small farmhouse and move all furniture in front of the doors and windows
 B) Ask for volunteers to implement corporate disaster guidelines
 C) Contact first responders and wait until help arrives
 D) Cut your hair into a multi-colored mohawk, put on shoulder pads, steal a muscle car and keep shooting until you go out in a blaze worthy of a Bon Jovi ballad

Chapter Ten

Magik followed Dani and their vegan mentor, Diana, into the restaurant. They sat down at the only open booth. All the others were taken and it seemed everyone was eating corn dogs. Dani sighed, Diana had chosen the wrong place; this joint looked like a meat house. The server was dressed in black, tattooed and had a silver septum ring. She came to their table with two different colored menus.

"We just need the vegan ones," said Diana.

The server only put the blue menus on the table. Dani held it up and smiled when she saw that it said *Hungry Tiger's Vegan Menu.*

"They have a separate vegan menu?" Diana smiled.

"Yeah, but it's Wednesday, so most people get the dollar twenty-five vegan corn dogs."

Dani laughed and looked around. "So some of those corn dogs are vegan?"

"All of them are, they only make them vegan."

At that point, a blood curdling falsetto scream carried through the speakers as a song by the thrash metal band, 3 Inches of Blood, played in the kitchen. Magik looked geeky bobbing his long, slightly mulletted Nordic locks to the thrash beat.

"This place is awesome," Magik smiled widely. "I can get a giant vegan pancake here and listen to metal."

"On the right night," Diana smiled. "So Dani, what happened at work today?"

"I thought I was losing my mind, so I need to ask you guys something." Magik held her hand, and Dani relaxed a bit. "My co-workers, especially the woman who sits across from me, she doesn't look good. She looked like, hell she acted like, a zombie."

The server came to their table and Diana ordered a dozen corn dogs and beers for the table.

"When you say she acted like a zombie, you mean she was spaced out."

"Her fucking skin was bluish-purple."

"Hmm, more *Dawn of the Dead*, than say, a gray, *Day of the Dead* tinge?" asked Magik.

"I don't know," said Dani.

Magik pulled out his iPhone. "I'm calling Bru-Dawg. He'll know."

"So I'm wondering, have either of you noticed anyone acting strange. It wasn't just her. All my co-workers were a little off."

Diana shook her head. Magik had been at home all day writing his graphic novel script in his office. So Dani knew his opinion didn't count for much. He probably was locked away until he biked over here.

Magik put his phone away. "He didn't answer. Look, you are not a big fan of your co-workers anyway," said Magik.

The server put down their drinks and a few seconds later a basket filled with corn covered veggie dogs was placed in front of them. Magik had a big smile on his face as he took his first bite.

"What's wrong with your co-workers?" asked Diana.

Dani didn't want to think of the office. Didn't want to think about work. She regretted bringing up the topic. Dani looked through the swinging doors into the next room. A man sat at the bar. He looked ill like Sally. His yellow eyes glowed from the darkened bar. He looked like a zombie, even in his tight-fitting ironic thrift store shirt and mustache. A neglected PBR sat in front of him, his mouth gaped and Dani guessed that he was groaning.

"They give her shit all the time for being vegan," said Magik.

"I warned you about that. The desert island question, the dreaded ex-vegan. I'm so glad I don't have to deal with that."

"How do you avoid it? It seems impossible to avoid that kinda crap."

"I work at a vegan bakery, so I suppose I am insulated."

Dani snapped back into the conversation. "Wait, no one at your work looked like a zombie today?"

"At the bakery? No, like punk rock kids maybe, but not zombies."

Diana laughed. Dani tapped her arm and pointed to the bartender. Intentionally messed-up hair, flannel shirt with rolled up sleeves, bandanna and purple skin. A woman sat at the bar snapping her fingers and the bartender just stared at her with yellow eyes.

"Yeah, like that, like a zombie."

"That's nothing," Diana smiled. "You know cocaine is super trendy with hipsters right now. He probably just did a line under the bar."

Dani took her first bite of a corn dog. It tasted greasy and good. Maybe her first assumption was right. It was in her head. She viewed the world so differently after having seen that *Earthlings* movie. Every time Sally sat at her desk eating a Big Mac it was hard not to think about the suffering. Watching most people eat their lunch was as grotesque to Dani as a scene in a movie of zombies ripping someone up and eating them.

"You know what?" Dani took another bite while her friends waited to know what. "Everybody acts like zombies are so scary and gross, but most people are flesh eaters. So the murder is done in secret and neatly packaged, but so what? Same thing."

Magik tipped his beer in salute and took a drink.

"It makes me so angry. Animals are dying while people like Sally pay ninety-nine cents a shot to get a piece of their burned flesh jammed on shitty bread. Sickening, I'm having a hard time dealing with it. In my head."

Diana nodded. "When you're first vegan it's hard to balance the knowledge, anger and emotions that come with it. It's heavy. Something you feel in your heart is murder, is normal and accepted. You are expected to respect people eating stuff that you know hurt an innocent animal."

Magik put his second empty stick back in the corn dog basket. "It's worse because people mock you for caring too," Magik wiped his hands and spoke with a little food still in his mouth. "Maybe if we got involved with some activism, as an outlet, that would help out."

"What do you mean get involved? Involved with what?" Dani said.

Diana swallowed her bite of food and nodded. "I know just the thing. Tomorrow the vegan mini-mall is having a gathering of activists. It's called the activist round-up. Organizers from all kinds of different animal rights groups set up a table and recruit volunteers."

Dani looked at the bar, she saw the zombie-looking hipster. He was wasn't a zombie and Dani knew it. He was just some dumbass. Dani needed some kind of change of pace. "Yeah, we'll check it out."

TEST

1. Better ways to keep Portland weird include:

A) Have every third light rail car be a dance party with space out lighting and glow in the dark seats

B) Require elected officials to drive dune buggies in a demolition derby that determines which neighborhoods get social service funding

C) Change the giant Made in Oregon *sign to say* Portland— the Home of the Meth Epidemic!

D) Brion James Film Festival (look him up)

2. *You can get $1.25 vegan corn dogs every Wednesday at:*
   A) Hungry Tiger, Too in Portland Oregon.
   B) You can't even get vegan corn dogs in San Francisco
   C) Not aware of any place in NYC to get them
   D) Not LA! I know, Portland is awesome

Chapter Eleven

Dani heard Crom barking down the street. He usually slept like a rock when Magik was out, but something had set the little guy off. When they pulled their bikes into the driveway, Crom stood straight up on the edge of the couch in the window and barked wildly. Dani leaned her bike up against the fence as Magik fumbled with his keys and talked to his dog through the window.

"Crom! What's wrong fella?"

"Ahhhh."

Dani jumped at the groan behind her. The Juggamom sat on the porch of the house, a cigarette burning in her fingers. Dani watched as ash almost the length of a finger blew off in the wind. Juggamom held the burning cigarette but never brought it to her mouth. The brown light from the Harrison's living room shined on Juggamom. Her skin looked pale, but it was hard to tell. She and Billy often painted their faces with clown makeup for concerts.

"Hello," Dani said and smiled.

Magik opened the door and Crom tried desperately to get past him, barking. Dani leaned on the fence.

"You feel alright . . ." Dani couldn't remember her name. This would have been a good time know her as anything other than Juggamom.

"Ahhhh," the Juggamom said.

The woman looked at her cigarette. Dani could tell she wanted desperately to put it in her mouth.

"I don't feel good . . ." the Juggamom said in a slow voice, just over a whisper, ". . . and shit."

"I think you need to see a doctor."

Behind her, Dani could hear Crom bark away. Headlights crossed over the front of the Harrison's house as someone drove around the corner. The momentary spotlight caused Dani to gasp. Juggamom's skin was purple, her eyes bright yellow. Brakes squealed. A white van stopped at the right spot to block both drive ways. A spotlight shined on them, Dani blocked her eyes but she had to turn away.

Magik stepped outside. Crom was back on top of the couch. The light faded slightly and two people dressed in full body plastic containment suits walked toward them. Dani watched them approach. One of the suits walked normally, the second trailed and dragged a foot slightly. As the suits got closer, the light from the house revealed a man and woman. The woman stayed back a step, but Dani could see anguish on her face, her skin color was the gray of puked-up Bob Evans biscuits and gravy.

"I'm Special Agent Jim Dumaski of the Seattle CDC Office. Do you mind telling me what you had for dinner?" The man spoke through a speaker on his suit.

Dani stepped back and looked at Magik. A second glance at Dumaski revealed he wasn't in great shape either. Under the plastic screen on the suit, the special agent looked sick.

"What did you have for dinner?" Dumaski repeated.

The Juggamom leaned forward. "Microwave Ribs dinner."

Dumaski looked at Magik and Dani.

"Uh corn dogs and fries."

"Were they Stress-Free label?" asked Dumaski.

Dani laughed. "No, we're vegan. They were soy, wheat or I don't know glue maybe."

Dumaski looked back at his partner, she shook her head. Dumaski walked toward Dani. "You don't feel ill at all?"

"No, but a lot of the people at my office. Well, they look terrible."

"Tell me, do your coworkers eat meat?"

"Oh, yeah," Magik said and giggled.

"Fuck," the two suited CDC workers said together. They both backed away toward the van.

"Wait. Can you help our neighbor?"

Jim Dumaski took his helmet off and released the trapped air. He took a deep breath of Portland air. "If I were you I'd stay home from work." Dumaski walked back to his van. "Come on Betty."

Betty didn't go on. She stood still. It looked like her face had aged a good thirty years under the glass of the containment suit. The speaker on her suit clicked on. "Ahhhh."

Dumaski cursed and pulled his partner back to the van. Magik tapped Dani on the shoulder.

"We need to walk Crom and get some sleep."

Dani nodded but watched as the CDC van peeled out. "Probably just a meth outbreak."

TEST

1. The reason CDC officials have been seen in Portland in containment suits is:

    A) They are keeping Portland weird, yo

    B) Indie rock hipsterness has gone airborne

    C) Containment suits are super good rain gear for biking

    D) Zombies!

2. Dani doesn't believe a zombie outbreak is happening because:

    A) It has become trendy to dress like a zombie

    B) The CDC agent did not tell her to shoot anyone in the head

    C) She hates irony

D) She had not seen one militia of rednecks shooting zombies for fun

Chapter Twelve

The vegan mini-mall was a landmark in Portland. A few blocks off of the street that separated the north and nouth sides of Portland east of the river, Diana referred to the area as the V-district. Not only did the mall have four dedicated vegan stores, but there was an entirely vegan collectively-run anarchist restaurant, the Red and Black Cafe, around the corner. Hungry Tiger, home of $1.25 corn dog and 40 cent tofu wing nights, was just a few steps further.

Geographically and socially speaking, this small section of Portland was the local center of the vegan community. A bakery, a clothing store, a tattoo shop and most importantly, the area's only entirely vegan grocery store, Food Fight. The bike racks were often full, and it was not uncommon to see vegan tourists from less vegan friendly cities outside the store posing for pictures.

A week after becoming vegan, Dani and Magik walked around Food Fight for the first time. It was incredible to shop for food in store where they knew they could buy anything. Marshmallows? Yeah, they have vegan ones. A cheese case filled not only with tofutti slices, but 12 dollar bricks of vegan blue cheese that had been imported from Scotland. Rare and hard to find vegan items were what they specialized in.

Dani wasn't surprised when they rolled up and saw all the bike racks loaded up. Bikes were locked to other bikes. They had to walk two blocks away to find somewhere to lock up. As they walked toward the mall, they heard lots of voices. People walked in and out of Food Fight.

After the night before, Dani breathed a deep sigh of relief when she noticed that everyone here was like-minded. She didn't have to worry about getting made fun of. The small store was packed with people. Card tables were set up in the small aisles and the first table Dani saw was In Defense of Animals.

"Hey, help us get fur out of Nordstrom forever!" The activist offered her a leaflet.

Another activist offered her more flyers. "We need your help to stop the Oregon Fish and Wildlife Service from shooting sea lions for eating fish."

"What? What the fuck are they supposed to eat?" said Magik.

Magik was disturbed by that idea and stayed to talk to the man. Dani walked to the next table. The Animal Defense League was organizing against hipster cook, Chef Panic, for selling foie gras at 11:50 Lounge. Dani signed up for that. Dani smiled as she passed the radical cheerleaders for animal rights who shook red and black pom-poms. They were recruiting cheerleaders to work the various protests around town. Try Vegan PDX were recruiting vegan veterans for their mentoring program and speakers for their annual Try Vegan Week. A woman who looked like she played bridge with Dani's mother handed her a flyer for Northwest Veg's annual Vegfest.

The key note speaker looked like Peter Sangar. His picture was a little less crazy-looking than when she last saw him. Dani looked through the stack of flyers, each one promoting a issue or an activist style that sounded interesting.

"I'm Sarah, I help organize the Vegfest." Sarah looked like a kindly grandmother to most but her smile and energy put Dani at ease.

"Dani."

"This is a cool event, huh?" Sarah motioned around the room.

Dani looked back across the room. She wasn't close enough

to hear him, but she knew Magik was making fun of Chef Panic at the ADL table. Three young vegan children begged their mother for another cookie by the door. And it hit Dani. It was the first time in weeks she had seen a room of healthy-looking people. The bus consistently held several coughing, nearly-dead looking workers who felt they had to go about their day despite obviously feeling like a warmed over butthole.

Sally was the first at work to look like she walked off the set of Romero movie. By the time she left work the other day, everyone looked ready to go to a dead movie casting session. Downtown's nearly catatonic homeless rate had increased, but many of the shambling slow walkers were drooling on their business suits.

It happened so slowly Dani had just figured it was in her mind. Here, with a room full of healthy and vibrant people, Dani realized just how bad things had gotten. The flesh-eating catatonic followers had taken over. They walked the streets everywhere.

"Hi, have you ever heard of Professor Gary L. Fonzie?"

Dani turned to see a woman a few inches shorter than herself holding out a business card. Dani looked at the card. *"Follow noted abolitionist philosopher and author of 'Animal Freedom – The Only Way, My Way,' Gary L. Fonzie on Twitter."* Dani flipped the card over and looked at the smiling picture. He looked normal enough.

"I'm Samantha. I'm with the Portland chapter of the Abolitionist Voice Committee."

Dani walked to the AVC table and scanned the leaflets. The titles surprised her.

What's wrong with PETA!
The problem with fur protesting.
Why your approach will fail animals.
Sea Shepherd – sure save the whales, but what about cows?

Dani looked at her confused. "I don't get it. You're against fur protesting?"

Samantha nodded.

"As professor Fonzie says, single issue campaigns can never work. We have to promote abolitionist vegan politics or we'll never make animal liberation a reality."

Dani looked around the room. "I get that. I mean, I'm new to all this vegan stuff, but I don't understand why you don't support the fur protests or . . ."

"As Professor Fonzie says in his book *Animal Freedom*," Samantha held a battered copy of the book. It looked as worn as a Bible thumper's *New Testament*. Samantha flipped the pages. It was highlighted and dog eared. Samantha pointed to a page. "Our goals should never be to ease suffering or reform suffering, as it only prolongs the suffering of animals in the long term."

Dani thought about it. Samantha believed in the power of the words to transform, so she let them hang in silence between them. Dani knew there was a truth to what she said. The Stress-Free Label products themselves had been a nightmare for animal advocates, except the ones who sold out and endorsed it. Dani agreed animals' pain and suffering were not the issue. Their use and exploitation were the problem. Welfare reforms wouldn't ease suffering and would only make matters worse in the end.

"Professor Fonzie just tweeted an hour ago. Did you know that the sales of meat, dairy and eggs have increased by twenty percent since the release of the so-called Stress-Free label products?"

"Yeah, it's awful." Dani looked back across the room at the In Defense of Animals table. An activist explained the Sea Lion campaign. Dani had seen a story on the news. Sea lions had been discovered catching salmon near the Bonneville Dam. It was like a sea lion buffet. Oregon Fish and Wildlife had decided they ate too many fish. Despite the fact that it was less than ten percent of the amount that humans fished out of the same river, and the ability of humans to manage their own share without violence, it was the sea lions who were on the firing line. The state had begun shooting and trapping sea lions every year.

"So wait," Dani pointed at the IDA table. "You still support their efforts to save the sea lions, right?"

Samantha looked at the IDA table and shook her head. "As Professor Fonzie says, single issue campaigns avoid the issue of species-ism. That needs to be our focus."

"So that's why you're against fur protesting . . ."

"Fur is not any more wrong than leather or wool."

"That's true, but . . ."

"As professor Fonzie says, it sends the wrong message that we value the lives of fur-bearing animals over the lives of egg-laying hens. That is the failure of single issue causes."

"I understand the argument, but I don't think a fur protest diminishes other issues. What about the sea lions?"

"Professor Fonzie says . . ."

Dani snapped. "I don't care what he says. He lives somewhere else, right?"

"Yes, but he would say this is a single issue campaign and..."

Dani stepped back a little. "I hope he wouldn't say that. Those sea lions need help and honestly you're the most single issued person here."

Dani walked past two tables and stopped when she got to a table with two guys wearing black bandannas around their faces. They had a used copy of Derrick Johnson's, *End the Game: A Call to Fight Civilization*, crappy-looking photocopies of the Animal Liberation Front Primer and a box of half-rotten vegetables. Dani stared at the eyes over the bandanna and laughed. The last thing it did was protect his identity. She would have known him from his campfire and dumpster sludge smell anywhere.

"Freddy?"

The two men looked at each other. Dani looked over at their e-mail sign up sheet. The group was called Anti-Civ Portland. Derrick Johnson was an author who toured the country promoting radical environmental views and considered the world's foremost advocate for being against civilization altogether. Dani had heard of him before, from Freddy. Freddy cleared his throat and spoke in comically deep voice.

"We're a local anti-civ group. We do survival skill shares and promote a primitive lifestyle."

"Freddy?"

"No Freddy here, I'm Mosspatch."

Freddy/Mosspatch reached up and pulled Dani away as she laughed. He kept the bandanna around his face.

"Dani, don't say my name."

"Uh, why is that?"

"Mosspatch is my earth name; I don't want anyone to know my slave name here."

Dani had her mouth open, ready for spitfire smart ass remarks, when the door swung open. Everyone in the small store turned to look at the wild-eyed middle-aged man in a suit. Dani was close enough to see his paper name tag: Don—President of Northwest Veg.

"THEY'RE COMING!"

Don turned and flipped the dead bolt. Chris, one of the Food Fight owners, grabbed his shoulders.

"Hey calm down, what's going on?"

Chris's wife, Emily, went to unlock the door.

"You can't!" Don laid himself against the door. The room was silent. The only sound, Don's heavy breathing. It was suddenly as comfortable as Michael Vick addressing a Dog Fancy convention. The silence ended with the sound of cell phones chirping away like crickets on a Midwestern summer night. The entire room of people opened or answered their phones. Dani was no different; her cell chirped. She flipped open her phone and saw a text message from Diana two doors away in the bakery.

ZOMBIES!

Dani was not the only one to get the message. A collective gasp followed by a few "What the fucks" circled the room. Don breathed heavy at the door. He nodded.

"I told you, it's bad out there."

A rotted face appeared in the window. A male zombie, mustached and dressed in a flannel with sleeves rolled up, walked into the window and groaned. Not just a zombie, a hipster zombie, banged at the glass. "Ahhhh!"

Chris, Food Fight's owner, turned back to the crowd. "Don't panic. We have a plan. Everybody to the back."

As the crowd huddled in the back, Chris, Emily, and their close friends unplugged the closest freezers and slid them across the floor to block the front door and windows of the store. Outside, the zombie crowd had grown to at least a dozen and more shambled toward them.

Magik sifted through the crowd holding his Blackberry. "Brent didn't answer, I heard the whole country has gone zombie!"

TEST

1. At this point the following people are already zombies except:
    A) Mister T
    B) Glen Beck
    C) Al Gore
    D) Woody Harrelson

2. The following store is not in the Portland V-district:
    A) Red and Black Café
    B) Food Fight grocery
    C) Sweet Pea Bakery
    D) Miller's Plumbing Gasket Emporium

Chapter Thirteen

The mini-mall was not a huge building. Each of the three open sides were surrounded by a growing crowd of groaning zombies. The back of the building butted up against a large firehouse. Dani watched Chris and his best friend, Mark, look out into the distance with binoculars. Magik and Dani talked themselves into the rooftop recon by suggesting that they were zombie experts.

Zombie Editor was on Dani's business card.

Dani talked out of her ass, but quoted things she heard at the Bru-Dawg team building exercise. She hoped she sounded knowledgeable and Chris seemed to buy it. They handed the binoculars to Dani and she took a look. After scanning in all directions, she winced. It was like flies drawn to a giant pile of shit. A magnetic pull dragged the zombies toward them from the surrounding blocks.

Across the river, sirens wailed and buildings burned. Closer, they heard screams from time to time. Mark and Chris had already walked to the other side of the roof where a steel ladder started twelve feet off the ground. They talked about cutting it off, but figured the zombies would not be climbing on each other to get to the ladder. Dani sighed with a deep sense of relief. Magik laughed at how relaxed she seemed.

"You seem a little relieved, considering there are zombies down there."

"I am. I was starting think I was going crazy."

Magik looked at his Blackberry. "It seems Portland, Burlington,

Vermont and the Bay Area have it the worst according to MSNBC."

Dani's eyes got wide, she thought about that CDC couple the night before. They asked Juggarnom if the microwave rib dinner was a Stress-Free label product. The three premiere cities for Stress Free products were San Francisco, Portland, and Burlington, Vermont. Dani ran the length of the roof. "Hey, we need to go talk to everyone. I know what caused this."

Dani was the first one down the small ladder from the roof. The majority of the people, about forty of them, had packed into an empty office space that was behind all the stores. As soon as Dani walked into the room she recognized Bru-Dawg, who was talking to Freddy, still clad in his bandanna. Dani had told the guys up on the roof that she wanted to tell everyone together. Dani walked to the middle of the room.

Samantha of the Abolitionists sat next to a man with Teva sandals and a slightly gray ponytail. He wore a wool-looking Mexican style poncho. The poncho had the words RAW VIBRATION spelled out with cartoonish vegetables. He was a raw fooder who ate only raw fruits, nuts, and vegetables. He was speaking to Samantha.

"You have to love yourself before you can love animals. It's less important what you eat than it is how you feel about it."

Dani whistled and stopped the conversation. "Is this everyone?"

Chris, Magik and Mark sat down. Everyone looked at Dani and she suddenly felt goofy with all eyes on her. "I think I know why this is all happening. I need to ask a few questions first."

People looked at each other and murmured.

"Have any of you noticed this illness sweeping through your work place or neighborhood?"

Almost everyone nodded.

"But it didn't happen to your vegan friends?" The murmurs picked up in intensity. Dani continued, "Who have you gotten calls from? Text messages? E-mails?"

"Just my vegan friends!" someone called, followed by several people saying, "Yeah!"

"Call them, text them and send e-mails while the systems are still in place. Tell them to hunker down. We are the only people left."

"How?" someone demanded.

"What happened?" another person yelled.

Magik stepped forward. "I think I get it. Last night, Dani and I saw two CDC agents. They asked what we ate."

Dani walked over to a dry erase board in the corner. She wrote "Stress-Free Label Products" on board.

Don from NW Veg nodded, Samantha from the AVC sighed and many put their hands over their mouths.

"The three cities to get the SF labels first have the worst outbreaks. The first zombie I saw was that Peter Sangar."

"The professor! No, he is vegan." Sarah, the grandmotherly vegan, said.

"No, he is not," Samantha shook her head. "Sangar endorsed Stress-Free eggs. Professor Gary L. Fonzie wrote a blog about it. As Professor Fonzie said, it is a clear sign that he supported the welfarist reforms that..."

"Shut-up!" one of the guys from ADL table said. Dani put her hands up.

"He was one of the first to eat Stress-Free eggs. He did it on TV, I saw it. So it makes sense that he would be one of the first full-blown zombies."

"Yeah he was in the store a few days back," Mark said, talking about Food Fight. "I just thought he was on some crazy bender. He looked fucked up."

"I don't understand," the Raw Vibration dude stood up. "It is painless for the animals. I got such great vibes about that stuff."

Don stood up and asked Dani for the marker. "I can explain. I'm a scientist."

Don drew a picture of a brain, with a stem. "Vir-Tech developed a drug that suppresses the cingulate cortex. It's my guess that concentrations of this chemical have built up inside the meat, dairy and eggs. Over time it would suppress large sections of the brain. The pain response would be gone. In a short time, it would kill parts of the brain while keeping other parts alive."

"So that's why they look dead?" Chris asked.

"Shit," Magik shook his head. "They're deader than Michael Jackson."

A silence came over the room. Dani stepped forward. "That drug was in everything: beef, chicken, eggs, cheese. Even fish farms were fed the stuff in fishmeal. The only people that were immune were vegans, and we are seriously out numbered."

"You make it sound like a battle," the Raw dude said as he sat back down and crossed his legs. "Life is not battle."

"I don't know dude, it sure looks that way now," Mark said and laughed. "We need to start killing zombies."

Mark was a vegan straight edger with twenty years of going to hardcore shows and four limbs full of militant vegan tattoos. He had seen Vegan Reich live when some of the younger activists in the room were learning ABCs from Bert and Ernie. He wasn't messing around.

"Killing? We're vegans, we don't even eat honey. How are we going to kill anyone?" Sarah the grandmother shook her head.

"Yeah, that's violence." Samantha stood up. "Professor Fonzie says violence runs counter to the vegan ethic of non-violence . . ."

"Stop!" Mark waved his hands. "The professor didn't factor in a zombie takeover."

Samantha was not moved. She shook her head and pointed at Mark. "Non-violence is the essential moral baseline for our struggle or we become like everyone else."

"Everyone else are zombies, Dumbass," Bru-Dawg said and laughed.

The tension was as thick 1990s-style vegan cake. Anger and divisions sprang up around the room. Magik raised his hand.

"Fact." He paused and took a breath as the room got quiet. "I would rather punch myself in the balls than go see *Cats* the musical."

Several people laughed, but most were confused. Dani walked over to Samantha and offered her a hand. They stepped over to the side a bit.

"Sam, can I call you Sam?"

Samantha nodded.

"Sam, non-violence is a great principle, but no one wanted to eat Gandhi's fucking brain, OK? Can we agree on that?"

Samantha looked around the room, confused. She looked like a cornered dog.

"No, Professor Fonzie says . . ."

Mark launched toward her but Freddy and Chris held him back. Mark kept yelling. "Don't you say his fucking name again, not one more fucking time! You hear me?"

Dani watched Freddy move back toward the back of the room with his other bandanna covered friend. They sat huddled in the corner by their boxes of rotting produce.

Bru-Dawg stepped forward. "Hey, Dani."

"Yeah, Bru."

"Well, it's just Brent. Your boss, I know he is probably totally Bub from Day of the Dead right now, but he had a lot zombie survival gear at his house."

Mark calmed down, heard this and walked toward Dani. "How far away?"

"Five minute drive," Magik said. "I went to a party there once."

Dani listened to them plan the mission.

"I've got a Glock 9MM." Mark said and lifted his shirt to show off his holster.

"Nice, dude." Magik nodded. "Yeah those have nice action. I've shot those many times."

Dani looked at him, confused.

Magik stepped back. "What?"

Dani pulled on Magik's arm.

"Since when do you know anything about guns?"

"Did you see my *Dawn of the Dead* biker gang targets in the basement?"

"I thought that was a joke."

"First in my class. I am super proud of those."

Dani shook her head. "You of all people should not be firing guns."

"Why? I'm good at it . . ."

"Why? You're asking why? How many times have you almost died?"

"All the more reason to master . . ."

Magik kept talking, but Dani's eyes caught Freddy in the back of the room, shaking. His friend also looked uncomfortable.

Dani walked past Magik and grabbed Bru-Dawg's arm. "You know Freddy right?"

"Uh, yeah, you mean Mosspatch? I've known him since Indiana. Stupid fucking name."

"I just remembered he's not vegan."

"No dude, He's a freegan."

Dani gasped. She walked toward Freddy/Mosspatch. Freegans were an interesting class of ex-vegan. They still often thought of themselves as ethically vegan, but would eat animal products as long as they were found in the trash. Dumpsters, trash cans. In their view it was ethically consistent to eat animal products as long as they were trash. They saw it as the most eco-friendly choice. Dani thought of it as unsustainable and parasitic, since it required the bad food habits of others to feed them.

Dani stood over Freddy. She looked in his box and saw it. Packages of Stress-Free label cold cuts from Trader Joe's. Freddy lifted his head and stared at Dani with bright yellow eyes. Dani stepped back and screamed. Freddy jumped up and moved awkwardly forward, his bandanna fell and revealed his rotten undead cheeks.

The whole crowd screamed and shifted. Dani fell back as Zombie Freddy moved closer on shaky legs, looking like a fawn learning to walk. Mark pulled out his handgun and ran through the crowd. A second wave of screams brought on another level of chaos.

"Cover your ears!"

Most of the crowd poured back into the bakery space. Mark watched Freddy come forward. Mark had shot at shooting ranges a million times, but this was different. Dani and Magik covered their ears but still it rang through the mini-mall sounding like bomb blast.

BOOM.

By the time Dani opened her eyes, Freddy's head had decorated the wall. Freddy's neck managed to hold on to his lower jaw and a couple teeth. His body hit the floor with a thud that no one heard thanks to the blast echo in their ears. Dani heard Mark speak but his voice sounded miles away.

"I always said they weren't vegan."

Dani turned her eyes toward Freddy's other freegan friend. He stood and walked toward them with his mouth open. Mark pointed his Glock at the freegan zombie. Samantha appeared in the doorway. Emily blocked her from coming in the back room.

"You don't want to see this, Sam," Emily pleaded with her as she held her back.

"Stop. Violence doesn't solve anything!" Samantha screamed.

"I disagree." Mark pointed the Glock at Freddy's mostly headless body. "I think it solves the freegan problem quite nicely."

Magik stepped behind Mark, who pointed his Glock at the second freegan zombie as it walked toward them.

"What are we gonna do, form some kind of vegan death squad?"

"Sounds good but," Mark stepped closer and put the gun on the zombie's forehead. "they're already dead."

"No!" Samantha screamed, but the gun went off and for the second time in the back room of the vegan mini-mall a gushy head, slightly out of date, exploded.

Mark wiped bits of zombie off his face and looked at Magik. He waited there until their hearing recovered from the damage the gun blast had done.

Dani walked over. "We need to make a plan to get to out of here and get some more weapons."

Magik agreed with Dani but turned and watched Samantha. Anger burned in her eyes. Magik wasn't worried. She was a pacifist; the only threat she posed was opening her mouth and annoying them until they went crazy.

Chris walked over, and scratched his beard. "I don't think many of them grasp the whole problem here."

Samantha walked back into the store. People in the crowd talked amongst themselves. Samantha cut them off. "Do you people know what just happened back there?"

Everyone heard the gun blast, everyone had seen Freddy's corpse walk around. It wasn't hard to do the math. More than one person cried. Several shook their heads in disgust. Even the people who understood had a hard time accepting it.

"They are talking about forming a death squad. The violence of the oppressor. Professor Fonzie warns about this. We have to stop the violence."

Chris and Magik shook their heads listening to Samantha continue to quote from professor Fonzie's book, she even stood upon a case of Tofutti cream cheese and held the book. Shaking and asking the survivors to join her, rise up against the tide of violence.

Mark and Dani ignored her ranting and looked out the window to the parking lot. Zombies were not as thick on the east side of the building in the parking lot, but they were making their way toward the door. A zombie came toward the window groaning. As he got closer, they could read the words on his ringer shirt: "Bacon is a Vegetable."

"Fuck that," Mark lifted his hand gun.

"Hey now," Dani pushed his hand down. "You only have eight

of those left."

Mark turned his back to the door and shook his head. Dani snapped her finger. Chris and Magik ran to the back door.

Dani spoke first. "I think we have to consider that Freddy and his friend were not the only non-vegans among us."

"Any of them could be infected," Chris added.

"That's not our only problem," Magik said. "Gandhi with a trust fund back there is really trying to turn people against us. Says we're violent."

"Maybe they should leave then," said Mark.

"No, we're going be all that's left, we have to stick together."

Magik looked at Dani and smiled. He never imagined her in this leadership role.

"What do you guys know about raw fooders?" Chris asked.

Dani and Magik both shrugged.

"There was a time when most of them were vegan. They still table at our conferences and kinda speak to the same crowd. Most of them do it for health reasons. They don't care about animal rights. You know they are all about raw milk now? The thing is, even if that stuff is not labeled, it's a slippery slope. You know they're cheating."

Dani closed her eyes and mildly hit her head back against the wall. She thought about all the ding dong hippie shit the raw fooder said about energy and vibrations. "I heard that Raw Vibration dude say it doesn't matter what you eat as long as you love yourself."

"He also said something about the good vibes he got from . . ."

They all jumped and followed Mark back into Food Fight. Samantha was on top of her Tofutti box. She shook her book and preached.

"Had we listened to Professor Fonzie and not the lies of the welfarist Stress-Free product supporters, this crisis would never have happened . . . ?"

Two people pumped their fists and listened. A few had fallen asleep, and Bru-Dawg sat behind her flipping sunflower seeds at her out of boredom. Mark walked past her to the Raw Vibration guy. He sat cross-legged, meditating. Mark shook his shoulder and when his eyes opened, yellow globes stared back at him. His hair had gone totally gray, his skin was not yet purple but it had changed.

Mark raised his gun. Samantha stepped closer.

"See how they resort to violence."

Samantha stepped in front of Mark's pistol.

"I can't let you do it."

"Ahhhh," the Raw Vibration dude groaned.

Dani looked at his face, his eyes were yellow, and he looked like Sally did in the early days of her illness. The Raw Vibration dude's half-zombie face rocked inches from Samantha's ass as she stood in defiance of his extermination.

"I knew it, you're all lizard people." Raw Vibration whispered. "All that cooked mush. Man, it changes you. Biogenesis. I got your number. The lizards taught you to cook that food, man."

"What the fuck is he talking about?" Mark asked, his pistol shaking in his hand.

"Doesn't matter. Violence is not the answer," Samantha said firmly.

Dani disagreed with what she was doing but she was impressed by the stand the young woman had taken. Raw Vibration dude groaned again.

Mark shook his head. "Move, Sam."

"No."

"It was just once," Raw Vibration dude whispered. "You have to love yourself, what's a slice or maybe four of cheese pizza? I had to love myself."

Raw Vibration dude lunged. He stuck his face against Samantha's tiny butt. She felt his teeth on her jeans. Mark pulled her forward and put the gun on the raw dude's head.

"Wait! Wait!" Raw Vibration screamed. "I'm not a zombie!"

"Not yet," Dani put her hand on Mark's shoulder. "Is there

somewhere we can lock him up?"

Dani helped lead the Raw Vibration dude to the bakery's walk-in freezer and managed to resist the urge to point out to Samantha that her pacifism almost came back to bite her in the ass.

TEST

1. A zombie's head explodes so easily because:

    A) It looks cool

    B) The body and head have already begun decomposing

    C) Zombies are stupid

    D) It is filled with ketchup and raspberries

2. Non-violence works great as a political tactic if:

    A) You can trust the morals of your opponent

    B) You apply for permits and protests in designated free speech zones determined by your opponent

    C) Undead hordes are trying to eat you

    D) You firmly have public support and control of the message

Chapter Fourteen

Zombies were gathered in front of the mini-mall banging on the windows rhythmically like a hanging sign blowing in a windstorm. Everyone became quiet, more than a few people hugged each other, and a few cried. Diana tried to keep a lid on the people at the bakery and made food for everyone. The plan was simple: get some rest and wait until the sun was up. In the morning, they would make a run for Brent's zombie apocalypse stash.

Diana traded a few text messages with the survivors at the anarchist restaurant up the street. They had a rough night, more windows and doors to secure. They didn't have any weapons and were having a collective meeting in the morning to decide if they were going to fight their way over to join the survivors at the mini-mall.

Dani helped Mark clean up what was left of Freddy. Magik pulled Freddy's legs and Dani marched holding a bucket of brains they had cleaned up with an old sock. She dropped the totally-lost sock into the bucket; it smelled like uncooked fish bodies. The longer the two zombies rotted, the more the room smelled like Pike's Market in Seattle.

Sarah, the grandmotherly vegan, followed them as they dragged the body toward the west side of the building. "Have you talked to any friends elsewhere?"

Dani shook her head. The only vegans she knew were here in the building. Her mother and brothers were probably on the streets searching for vegans to eat as they spoke.

"There are survivors all over town," Sarah held up a piece a paper. "We have made a list of those we have contacted by phone or e-mail, a couple hundred already."

Magik took a deep breath and stopped at the side door on the sidewalk. Dani set down the bucket and smiled at Sarah.

"That sounds good. So the internet is still up?"

"Seems like it. And Dani," Sarah smiled with a strange sense of pride, "we posted around about your theory and it looks like you're right."

Dani didn't like being right because it meant a lot of bad news for the world. Dani unlocked the side door and looked out. The closest zombie was twenty feet away at the corner. Dani laughed when she saw the stop light and the crosswalk tick away like no apocalypse had happened. She turned back to Magik, ignoring Sarah for a moment.

"Zombie. Twenty feet at nine o'clock, do this quick."

Dani opened the door and Magik pulled the zombie body out into the street. Sarah held the door and Dani dumped the bucket of brain into the gutter and heard the slush drain toward the sewer. The zombie at the corner barely turned around. Dani looked up and saw faces watch her from the kitchen of the Red and Black Cafe. Zombies surrounded the restaurant but only one punk rock looking mohawked zombie stood by the back door. The anarchists would only have to run half a city block.

Bru-Dawg whistled and Dani headed inside before he shut and locked the door.

Bru-Dawg shook his head at Magik. "You know, I don't think I've ever thought about how bad zombies would smell."

"I have," Magik said as he wiped his hands on a rag. "I mean, that first scene in *Day of the Dead*, it just looks hot and humid."

"Yeah, I suppose you're right." Bru-Dawg laughed, despite the smell.

Sarah hugged Dani. She looked over the older woman's shoulder and smiled at Magik. "We can't lose you Dani." Sarah whispered in her ear.

Dani laughed.

"People are scared. Most of the survivors are alone, in small groups. Besides us and the PETA headquarters, there are only a few groups of survivors working together."

Dani put her arm around Sarah. "Look, we still have the internet. We need to plan. Portland has one of the largest vegan communities in the world, right?"

"Yeah," Sarah said with smile on her face. She wanted to be led, to be told what to do.

"Get online. You start searching Google for supplies. Lead the survivors here. Put together an effort and you get them here."

"Portland?"

"Yep, we'll organize our community over the next couple weeks. We'll clean up the city, clear the zombies. Get it ready. We have more than enough water and a long growing season. If we're going to rebuild we need to start here."

Sarah smiled at Dani with the same goofy smile Jewish parents have during their child's bar and bat mitzvah. Pride and joy smushed in a sickeningly syrupy ball of corniness. "Yes ma'am," Sarah said, and pumped her fist. She ran back to the storeroom.

Bru-Dawg followed behind her, already sending a message on his phone.

Magik saluted Dani. They laughed and shared a kiss that would have been more romantic if they didn't both smell like blown apart zombie brain. Magik ran his fingers through Dani's hair, wiping away a gooey piece of Freddy's cerebral cortex.

She smiled at him. "Big day tomorrow. Let's get some sleep."

Dani awoke to the sun coming through the back room window. It shined on her face. Even through the glass it felt warm. When her eyes opened, the glass window above her was filled with a hipster zombie staring at her. He wore a "Bacon is a Vegetable" t-shirt and a string of drool hung from his mouth like bungee cord.

Magik squeezed Dani tight as he awoke. He put on his glasses and saw the zombie clearly.

"Well hello, Sunshine." Mark walked into the back room, He had on an Earth Crisis sweatshirt with the hood up, large construction gloves with giant X's marked on them, and a holster with his Glock on the belt of his dessert camo shorts. He clapped. "Rise and shine, it's time for the war."

Chris, Emily and Diana walked in behind him.

Diana held up her iPhone. "They took at vote at The Red and Black. They are coming here."

Dani nodded. "That's perfect, a distraction. Can they be ready in five?"

Five minutes it was.

The anarchists were armed with wood boards MacGyvered with nails at the end. One lone punk rocker zombie waited at the bottom of three concrete steps at their back door. They'd watched the zombie try to figure out the stairs all night.

The plan was they would open the back door, slam a nail board into the zombie and run for the mini-mall where Emily would open the door. This would attract the attention of the zombie hordes. Fifteen seconds after the door at the cafe opened, Dani and her team would go.

The signal was given. Dani heard screams from the far side of the mini-mall and watched the seconds tick off. Fifteen seconds suddenly seemed impossibly long. The parking lot zombies all walked away toward the open food source on the other side of the building, except for the bacon-is-a-vegetable hipster, who stared in the window, inches outside the door, his drool now to the pavement.

"We can't wait," Dani said and Mark nodded. Dani opened the door and the hipster zombie reached and grabbed her hair. Mark pushed his pistol out the door. The boom was so close to Dani's head she screamed, but she couldn't hear herself. She felt the zombie's grip loosen. She watched the zombie spin around with a huge chunk of his head missing. If he were aware enough to notice, he would have been pleased his ironic mustache was intact as his body hit the parking lot. Two zombies turned back toward them.

Magik and Bru-Dawg each grabbed an arm and pushed Dani toward Mark's car. Dani's hearing felt like it was being processed by a wah-wah pedal. The first sound she could make out was the door shutting behind her as the three of them crowded into the back seat of the Prius. Mark passed his gun back to Magik, who survived a gunshot wound when he was fourteen and decided he needed to master a weapon. Now was his first chance to test his skills.

Mark pushed the power button and waited for the on-board computer to come on as the small car was surrounded by zombies. "Take out one, see if that scares them."

The sunroof rolled open. Magik stood tall and pointed at a zombie crawling up on the hood of the car. He pointed and said his farewell to bullet number seven. The head exploded into flying brain matter. The car didn't roar to life; instead its hybrid engine quietly clicked. Mark saw that it was on. He put the car in gear and backed up, bumping over the zombie behind them. The zombie body on the hood rolled off onto a pile of disoriented undead.

Diana fought away zombies with a straw broom. Chris pulled the massive garage door down as a fresh horde of zombies ran toward them.

"We need some help out here!" Diana screamed, but it was too late. Magik pointed his gun at the zombies but failed to line up his shot in time. They watched a zombie bite into Diana's arm. Dani screamed and punched the window of the Prius.

"No!" Bru-Dawg pulled Dani back before she kicked at the window. "Oh shit. Get out of here!" Bru-Dawg yelled.

Chris had no choice—he dropped the garage door. Diana pushed herself into the zombies like she was stage diving at a show. She knew she was a goner.

"Magik! Take her out!" Dani yelled but didn't look.

Magik pointed the pistol. The zombie horde was three thick, all fighting for a piece of Diana. Dani knew in her heart he didn't have a shot; even through her tears, there was no way to even see Diana.

"I can't!" Magik slammed his fist on the roof.

They could hear her screams. Diana wailed from the bottom of the horde as they tore her to shreds.

Bru-Dawg leaned back in the seat. "Choke on it," Bru said just over a whisper.

"Mark, get us out of here!" Dani yelled.

"Fuckers," Mark messed with his iPod connected to the dash. "Normally, I would listen to *Slayer* on a killing spree." Mark found the song he wanted. The guitar pounded through the car.

"Oh god," Bru-Dawg shook his head.

Earth Crisis–*Wrath of Sanity* blasted though the car as they pulled out of the parking lot as fast as the hybrid would pick up.

The drive through the Southeast side of Portland was surreal. There were not as many zombies out on the streets as they expected. Magik never used bullet number six getting them out on the street past the mini-mall. The front bumper was stained with smashed zombie heads, but they were able to save the bullet. As they cleared the block, they went almost half a mile before they saw the next zombie.

They drove up Belmont Avenue and saw some zombies stumble out of the Zupan's gourmet grocery. The store had been one of the first to promote the early premiere of Stress-Free label meats and cheeses. The store was now filled with zombies who made it through the automatic door at the front. The city was still; there were a few crashed buses, and the occasional undead walker, but mostly it seemed quiet.

Mark drove, shaking his head.

Bru whistled, then asked what they were all thinking: "Where the fuck are all the zombies?"

Mark turned down the music as they turned on to 39th Ave. They turned onto Brent's street. One lone zombie, an overweight man in tennis shorts and no shirt, walked slowly, a block away. They pulled up across the street from Brent's house. Three cars filled the driveway.

"Shit," Bru-Dawg said and pointed. "Luke and Keith's cars."

"They must have come here to ride out the storm," said Magik.

"Were they vegan?"

Bru-Dawg laughed. "Keith put sausage on his waffles."

"Then they're dead now."

Dani opened the door. Her ears still rang from the gun blast. She pulled out her ear plugs. The neighborhood was quiet. A mild breeze blew the trees around. Leaves were coming back after the winter. Clouds were coming from the west. She heard a faint zombie groan followed by a pounding, slow rhythm.

The house banged. It was as if someone inside was knocking on the door to be let out. Dani walked toward the house. She heard a similar pound at the house next door. A third pound on the door at another house down the street. Dani looked inside a small window beside the door. Two zombies, husband and wife, were at the door. They smelled Dani and groaned pathetically. They knocked into the door again. They were drawn to her but didn't know how to open the door.

Magik stepped out of the car and laughed. Front doors up and down the street were thumping but the zombies locked inside couldn't manage the handles. The one zombie on the street groaned and marched toward them, hands in garden gloves raised high.

Mark stepped out and gripped his Glock. "Should I save number six?"

"Yep." Bru-Dawg stepped out with a baseball bat. He was a librarian, but he had years of customer service frustration built up inside. He took a swing directly at the zombies head. The thump of the bat and skull made Bru laugh. The zombie fell. Bru lifted a screwdriver and pushed it into the fallen zombie's ear.

"*Dawn of the Dead*! Nice kill!" Magik said and laughed.

Bru-Dawg pushed the screwdriver slowly into the ear. He was surprised how gross it felt as the screwdriver disappeared into the head like shovel in a snow bank. The zombie stopped squirming. It was Bru-Dawg's first zombie kill. Magik and Mark had already begun to compete and the score was even.

Dani walked up to Brent's house. She hadn't been there yet but it had been described to her. Brent's zombie survival gear was hidden in the basement. The same room where his flat screen TV and zombie DVD, VHS and Blu-ray collection were stored. Luke had said it was like museum of zombie culture.

Dani had to get on her tiptoes when she looked in a window on the door. She didn't see anyone. She put her hand on the door. It was unlocked. She looked back at Mark. He nodded. She opened the door and Mark jumped in with his gun held high.

The house was clean, quiet, and felt empty. Magik stepped in and pointed to the basement door. It was shut. Behind the door they could hear music blasting. Dani knew right away, in all its '70s electronic glory, the Goblin soundtrack to *Dawn of the Dead* blasted from beyond the basement door.

"He's down there, for sure." Magik shook his head.

TEST

1. The zombie apocalypse might be worse if:
    A) The soundtrack was scored by Foghat
    B) We didn't have cell phones and the internet
    C) Zombies were faster and smart enough to open doors
    D) Anyone at Fox News survived

2. The following '70s TV stars are all now zombies except:
    A) Charo
    B) Dirk Benedict
    C) Rerun from What's Happening
    D) John Schneider of The Dukes of Hazard

Chapter Fifteen

"Ok, I'll go first," Mark whispered.

Magik shook his head. "I should go first." His booming voice freaked everyone out. Magik laughed. "Don't need to whisper. They're fucking zombies."

Bru-Dawg laughed and suddenly Mark felt stupid. They all laughed, tension relieved for a moment. Magik grabbed the pistol. He had been here before, so it made sense that he would go first. He opened the basement door. The basement was lit with a brownish tint. The only light was *Dawn of the Dead* playing in the back of the large room on a large flat screen TV. Magik could tell instantly from the sound that it was the gas station scene near the beginning of the movie.

He walked down the steps slowly and more of the room came into focus. He had six bullets—two for each of them if it was Brent, Luke and Keith. Dani followed behind him. Behind her, Bru-Dawg stepped carefully with the bat.

Once Magik put his foot on the carpeted floor, he heard a sound behind him. It was too late, but he remembered the area under the stairs. The stairs were flat, open platforms.

"Ahhhh!"

A hand reached through the steps and grabbed Magik's left leg. Magik fell toward the steps. A pair of lips and teeth closed down on the fat of his calves. Why had he worn shorts?! Magik screamed as blood sprayed on the steps. Bru-Dawg took the bat and stabbed it under the steps, hitting the zombie underneath. Dani screamed and looked down. A zombified Luke, whose greatest achievement in life was a *Raptor Attack* sequel, bit down onto Magik's leg.

Dani grabbed the pistol out of Magik's hand and pointed the gun between the steps at Luke. Dani couldn't help in that moment but think about Luke. He had been an asshole to her ever since the day he found out she was vegan. Jokes about the food chain and tofu were cracked daily. Almost every interaction was some kind of immature routine about her being vegan. Stupid questions about what she would eat on deserted island.

Luke's eyes burned yellow. Magik's blood dripped from his mouth. Dani cringed as her boyfriend screamed again. Mark yelled above her.

"Shoot!"

Dani pointed, closed her eyes, and squeezed. *BOOM!* Bullet number six collided with Luke's nose at hundreds of miles per hour. Bones, face, and brain all mashed together. Luke's body dropped to the floor with a splash.

Magik also fell to the floor and gripped his leg. Dani handed the smoking gun to Bru-Dawg who passed it like a hot potato on to Mark. Dani hugged Magik.

"Oh shit. Brent."

A zombie Brent walked toward them in the light cast from the movie. His face was dead and rotting, but his body was covered in bullet belts and two holstered guns. He had tried to protect himself from the zombie apocalypse. He fought desperately to keep out the monsters, but the real terror attacked him from inside his bowels. He couldn't escape what he ate.

Magik tried to put weight on his leg but fell over. Dani rushed to his side. Mark kept his eye on Brent. Magik gripped his leg and felt the blood pour. He had watched this scene in countless zombie movies. He knew what would happen. Magik coughed as he spoke.

"Today is a good day to die."

"Stop it," Dani shook her head. "We don't know that yet."

Bru-Dawg whispered to Mark, "Dude. Who quotes Klingons when they're dying?"

"It's an old Native American saying," Mark whispered back.

"No, I was quoting Klingons." Magik said.

"See," Bru-Dawg shook his head. "Nerd."

Dani squeezed Magick's hand. "You can't die. How many near death experiences have you survived?"

Magik thought about it. "Including when I reworked the wiring at the house last week, seventeen times."

"This will be eighteen."

Magik shook his head. Brent groaned zombie-style as he stepped closer.

Mark leaned down toward Magik. "Hey, I know he was your friend and this is a sucky time, but do you mind if I go ahead and blow off this fucker's head?"

"No, go ahead."

Magik and Dani covered their ears. Brent put his hands up.

"Ahhhh!"

BOOM.

Dani supported a bandaged Magik as they walked into Brent's bunker. He didn't have much time left, she could already tell his skin had gotten pale. Was he dying from the loss of blood or was he in the first stage of turning into a zombie? Either way, it wasn't good.

Magik wanted to see what Brent had. They pushed the button to the bunker. The door sounded like the giant blast doors in *Aliens* as it opened. Knowing Brent, he probably had the exact sound sampled and playing on speakers. The room looked like Schwarzenegger's tool shed in *Commando*. The only difference, the old faded and framed *Night of the Living Dead* poster in the back of the room signed with, "Stay scared, George A. Romero."

Bru-Dawg stepped inside and looked around. "Shut up!"

Dani wasn't sure if he was impressed by the weapons or the poster.

"When did he get that?" Bru-Dawg looked back at the mostly headless body of his buddy Brent. "Dibs on the poster."

Magik walked up to a large machine gun and patted it. "Now I know Chuck Norris jumped out of the water firing one of these in *Missing in Action,* but that's impossible. Heavy gun."

"Badass," Mark laughed.

Magik handed a rifle to Dani. "You ready to learn about guns?"

"Why me?"

"You need to take charge. It will help if you can take out zombies yourself."

Dani took a hold of the rifle at looked at Magik. He nodded. She could see in his eyes that he had something planned. Dani thought of Bru-Dawg's words to her before this all started. *Blaze of glory dude, Blaze of glory.*

"Hey guys!"

Dani followed Bru-Dawg's voice out into the home theater in the basement. The bathroom door shook. Something bumped into it, a few seconds of silence and again a bump.

"Keith?" Bru-Dawg asked.

Keith responded. "Ahhhh!"

This little nerdy dipshit was a textbook model of the Napoleon Complex. He was nothing but a jerk to Dani from the minute he found out she was vegan.

"Give me the gun," Dani demanded as zombie Keith shook the door.

Dani felt self-assured as Mark put the Glock in her hand.

Bru-Dawg opened the door. Keith almost fell over, but walked with his zombie arms out.

Mark stood behind Dani. "See the white dot on the end of the barrel? Put that where you want the bullet to go."

Dani centered the sight on Keith's forehead.

"Don't be afraid tighten up for the kickback."

BOOM!

Keith's body fell back into the TV still playing *Dawn of the Dead*. The flat screen fell over and smashed on top of Keith's head. Sparks flew for a second, but Bru-Dawg stomped out the small fires that sparked up on the carpet. Magik walked out of the room with two bullet belts, an Uzi and a sawed off shotgun in a holster tied to his leg.

Bru-Dawg nodded in approval. "Fuck yeah, blaze of glory."

TEST

1. The movie with the highest fictional body count is:
> *A) Rambo IV*
> *B) Friday the 13ᵗʰ: Jason Goes to Hell*
> *C) Commando*
> *D) Invasion USA*

2. Goblin was known for doing the musical scores for the films of this director:
> *A) Ricky Schroder*
> *B) Dario Argento*
> *C) Alan Smithee*
> *D) Michael Bay*

Chapter Sixteen

They loaded Brent's pickup truck with as many weapons as they could fit. The zombies up and down the street smelled them and heard their movement and the pounding on the doors became incessant. Mark called the mini-mall. They cleared the loading area near the large garage door to the the parking lot. The parking lot had more zombies than ever according to reports. Dani knew they would have a fight on their hands.

Magik helped Bru-Dawg load the pickup. They talked about '80s action movies and guns. Brent apparently only bought weapons he had seen Norris, Stallone or Schwarzenegger endorse.

Mark and Dani sat at the kitchen table and drew up a plan. Mark waited to speak until Magik left the room.

"We have to talk about him."

"I know," Dani said and leaned back in the chair.

"Being vegan doesn't make you immune to zombie bites. He is already slowing down."

"I said I know," Dani looked outside and watched the two men load the truck. Magik talked, Bru-Dawg laughed. Magik's smile killed her inside.

"He's not coming back with us," said Mark. "What he does is his choice."

Magik and Bru-Dawg walked into the house, and laughed until they saw the looks on Mark and Dani's faces. Magik nodded and walked back down into the basement.

Dani drove Magik in the pick up truck behind Mark and the Prius. They didn't say anything. Dani didn't cry until they made the final turn. Mark slowed down the car when they got to the spot Magik requested.

"You sure about this?" Dani asked as she put the truck into park.

Magik shook his head. "Of course not."

Magik leaned over and kissed her. Dani grabbed the back of his neck, his lips were cold, not as cold as ice but chilled. The skin on the back of his neck under his long hair was stiff like concrete on its way to becoming solid.

"It feels right."

Magik gave her a last kiss on the forehead and stepped out in the street. "I love you, and think of it this way: you have a chance to make a better world."

Dani closed her eyes but the tears burst through. When she opened her eyes he stood there looking like a cartoon. The wind blew through his mullet making him look like Thor, and he was armed like Rambo.

Mark honked his horn.

"Go!" Magik said and loaded a shell into his shotgun with a snap.

Magik's Blaze of Glory Interlude

Magik watched the pickup truck head down Belmont. The wind whipped the silent street. A tumble weed rolled past Magik's feet and he felt like he was in some kind of post-apocalyptic western. There were no tavern doors to swing in the wind, just the automatic doors of a market. He laughed as the doors scanned him and swooshed open. It was a good death, one he could laugh about.

Magik walked into the Zupan's market. The prices at the store were insane. You couldn't buy a package of noodles for under three bucks. He used to live down the street and out of laziness he had shopped here a few times. There was not a product that was inexpensive in the whole building. He fucking hated this store.

He stepped farther inside the building. Each of the aisles was filled with zombies. The automatic door had let them in. They didn't smell him because Magik was on his way to being one of them. They kept walking the aisles aimlessly bypassing over-priced food. They would do it until they rotted apart all over the floor.

This was a mission of mercy. He needed to let them know he was here. Magik scanned the front of the store. They had a large sign just inside the door. "100 % Stress-Free label products." Magik looked at the sign and fired his shotgun. The sign exploded and the plastic board holding it burst into a thousand pieces.

The zombies didn't stop, and only one turned around. Most kept marching around the store. Magik turned his iPod on to Slayer. The song was *Reign In Blood*, when the sample of thunder gave way to thrashing metal he ran at the meat counter. A zombie in a white apron was stuck behind the counter groaning.

"Ahhhh."

Magik fired one round through the meat case into the zombie's gut.

"Ahhhh."

The zombie's Meat Department hat fell off. He had a small bald spot on his head. Magik aimed with one eye and performed a Magik Trick. *BOOM* ! The disappearing head. The meat case dripped rotting brain chunks and thick, gravy-looking blood.

Magik turned to a zombie woman walking past the cheese case. "You're welcome!"

Magik lifted an Uzi and sprayed bullets up the cheese aisle. Chunks of moldy dairy and zombies flipped into the air before three zombies walking in two directions hit the ground. Magik ran past them into the frozen food aisle and saw a dozen zombies march toward him.

Magik jumped in the crowd and reached into his jacket pocket. The grenade felt heavy in his hand. Zombie hands reached across his body, the zombie fingers felt like bugs crawling on his skin. Magik pulled the pin and squeezed the grenade.

"Eat this you zombie fuckers!"

The zombies burned away before the natural gas powering the freezers ignited. Magik laughed as the store burst into flames.

Dani swerved the truck when she heard the boom. She looked in the rear view mirror and saw smoke rise over Southeast Portland. Her emotions pulled at her but she felt a responsibility to rise above it all and be a leader.

They were passing a cemetery only a few blocks from the mini-mall when Dani saw another zombie. It was a frumpy middle-aged woman. She dragged her foot down the sidewalk painfully slow, as all zombies do, followed faithfully by her little white dog. The dog dragged its leash behind it, looking from time to time at its person's dead face.

Dani slowed the truck down and honked her horn. Mark stopped the Prius, but had to reverse. Dani got out of the truck and put a bullet in the chamber of the handgun she'd picked out in Brent's man-cave. She lifted the pistol. The tiny white dog barked. The zombie woman lifted her arm, suddenly energized by the presence of three living people to eat.

Dani pointed the gun; the sound of the dog barking was too much. This little dog was loyal and protective of this woman who had cared for her. Dani was surprised the smell had not scared the dog off.

She couldn't do it front of the dog. Dani lowered the gun. "Take the puppy."

Bru-Dawg opened the back door to the Prius. "Here doggie."

The little white terrier looked up at her person with a questioning look. It was as if it was asking, *'is it ok?'*

"Ahhhh!" The hungry zombie replied.

The little dog ran into the car and Bru-Dawg shut the door. Dani lifted the pistol. The zombie wasn't coming fast, all Dani had to do was keep backing up. Dani could sense Mark get nervous behind her. He wanted to keep moving. This woman was more than a zombie to Dani now. This zombie had loved that dog in life, and even as her body was dying, she took that little lady out for a walk. It was during the walk she had passed away.

"She's already dead, just finish it."

"Fuck." Dani pulled the trigger. The head blew apart. The terrier barked like crazy.

"We taking Muffin?" Bru-Dawg walked up behind Dani. "That's the name on her tags."

Dani looked back at Muffin standing up in the window, panting. She needed to get Crom. Everyone back at the mall would have dogs and cats to take care of. They were vegans, after all is said and done, most would have a house full of animals.

"Yeah, of course we are." Dani put the pistol back in her holster.

Mark looked at Muffin in the back seat. "Why don't the zombies eat animals?"

Dani shrugged and walked back toward the truck.

Bru-Dawg smiled. "Pretty cute dog." Bru-Dawg opened the passenger side door. "You ever see *A Boy and His Dog* with Don Johnson? That is a weird movie."

Dani put the truck in drive and hit the gas. The plan had changed. The important thing was that she had one.

TEST

1: Zombies only eat human animals because:
    A) They are dumb
    B) The zombification process creates an internal desire to

consume living flesh in an attempt to recapture the lost sense of life
      C) Why do Klingons suddenly have bumpy foreheads and why do you care
      D) Because I said so

2: The best thrash metal song to listen to while dying in a blaze of glory is:
      A) Testament – "Into the Pit"
      B) Metallica – "Battery"
      C) Sepultura – "Arise"
      D) Slayer - "Reign in Blood"

Chapter Seventeen

The zombies were gathered in the parking lot on the east side of the mini-mall. Mark called Chris to make sure they were ready to open the garage door. Bru-Dawg totally failed his first shooting test, so he took over driving. The Prius plowed into the parking lot blasting "Angel of Death" by Slayer. The opening scream of the song was still going when Mark stood in the sunroof and opened fire. The AK sang and bullets rained.

Zombie bodies shook. Brain and mush sprayed across the parking lot. When the first zombie bounced off the hood of the Prius, Dani pulled the truck in behind. Dani watched the zombies bounce off the hood of the truck and she had a light bulb moment. That is why cars in post-apocalypse movies are all souped-up with crazy equipment—for ramming.

The zombies still standing turned on the car. The large door opened up and the Prius rolled inside, dragging a zombie woman in tall boots and giant oversized bug glasses clinging to the outside mirror. The truck pulled in behind, barely fitting in the garage. Dani could hear screams inside the grocery store before the garage down slammed down. Mark leaned over the car and shot a single bullet into the head of the trendy-booted woman.

Two zombies had walked into the garage before the door came down. One reached out for Chris, the store owner. Dani stepped out and pointed her pistol. The first shot was wide. Chris ran away and the second shot blew off a chunk of the zombie's shoulder. It had been a boy, a teenage punk rocker wearing a jean jacket with cut-off sleeves. His toothpick arms were outstretched as he marched mindlessly toward Dani's flesh. Her aim had not improved. Dani walked up to him. His yellow eyes grew wider. That reaction took Dani by surprise, but her pistol was already on his forehead. The teenage zombie grabbed at her arms and opened wide for a bite. *BOOM!*

The other zombie moved a little faster than most. He wore a tight shirt and leggings, all neon. Dani had seen this guy before, riding a glow-in-the-dark bike up and down Alberta Street.

Bru-Dawg laughed and pointed. "Oh dude, let me shoot him, I always hated that fuckin' dork."

Mark moved around the Prius to get a good shot. Emily shut the door to the grocery store. Inside, Samantha began again to preach non-violence. The neon zombie headed toward Emily, the scent of her flesh luring him. Chris pointed at the neon zombie.

"Kill that fucking thing."

Mark pointed and aimed. Emily was right behind it, he couldn't risk the bullet going through the head toward Emily.

"Emily, get down."

Emily dropped, Mark squeezed, and the zombie's head disappeared in a hail of brain chunks. In the following silence, the groans of zombies on the other side of garage door increased like their volume knob had turned up to eleven.

"Anything happen while we were gone?"

"We had another freegan to kill, with a shovel."

Mark shook his head. "What about the Raw Fooder?"

"He is full zombie. There is another woman who has been raw for a few months, but she is vegan and fin," Emily said before she put her shirt over her nose. It did little to lessen the stink of zombie guts on the floor.

Mark quoted Han Solo in response. "I know, I thought they

smelled bad on the outside."

Chris waved Dani over to their discussion. "People want a plan. There is a tech nerd named Travis, he set up a web cam and we're going to stream a meeting on the internet. We've got groups in Chicago, LA, and a couple on the East coast forming."

"I have a plan but let's talk about it as a group. I don't want to be leader. I think we can avoid them for awhile."

Samantha was the only person who refused to attend the meeting. She declared that they were worse than welfarists. To abolitionists, "welfarist" was pretty much the same thing as calling someone asshole or douche bag. Sam sat in the corner with her laptop, emailing others from her national group who had survived the day after. A few had told her that things had changed and they were killing zombies. Very few still remained as committed to non-violence once their parents or co-workers turned purple and tried to eat them.

The professor had not responded to her messages. Sam feared the worst but vowed to keep his message alive.

The meeting took hours. Dani had a hard time keeping all the subcultures and their demands straight. The surviving primitivists argued against putting back together another system. The PETA soccer moms suggested that they try to rebuild the country; apparently Dennis Kucinich was the only surviving member on the three branches of government. PETA was planning an inauguration ball, with a red carpet of surviving celebrities. The vegan straight edgers were ready to kill zombies—that took little convincing. The raw fooders wanted to focus on going south and chilling out. The anarchists insisted that every voice be equal, that a system of consensus be set up.

Dani agreed with the anarchists for the time being, but worried the irrational pacifists would suggest that they leaflet the zombies instead of turning them into mush.

"Can they be educated?" asked an anarchist from the video feed in D.C.

"Educated to do what?" Dani shook her head. "Not want to eat humans? Look, their brains are mush, they are already dead. Maybe we need a new word. I mean were not killing them really."

"You sound like a welfarist," Samantha said and guffaws circled the room. "Free-range, Stress-Free, livestock, all these words redefining and cleaning up the act of murder and enslavement. That is what it is. You can change the words, you try to make it look pretty, but violence is violence."

"The old world killed those people. They killed themselves," Dani said and the confidence in her voice surprised even her.

"Excuse me." Ingrid Newburry, the British born president of PETA raised her hand on the video feed from their headquarters in Virginia. Dani cringed, she hoped Ingrid wasn't going to suggest they would rather be naked than kill zombies, or that the cause would be best supported by women in bikinis. "We at PETA believe that we can reduce the suffering by rounding up the zombies and painlessly putting them to death with gas."

"Like all the puppies you killed in your shelter."

"Our agenda is simple; open the humane death centers and President Kucinich's inauguration."

"Nobody voted on anybody yet," someone from Chicago yelled.

The yelling began, everyone talked over each other.

Dani looked at Mark who shook his head in disgust. Dani stood up and whistled. "Look we don't have time for this. We need leaders in the time being."

"We heard that before from Castro, Lenin," one of the Anarchists said.

"We need centers where we can pool our resources." Dani ignored the snide comment. "One on the East Coast. Virginia has a good growing season. Maybe farther south in North Carolina. Chicago in the Midwest, and here on the West Coast."

"Why Portland?" a person from L.A. asked.

"We have a huge vegan community. We probably have the most survivors," said Emily.

"We have better growing weather too." Dani walked closer to the camera. "Look these zombies are dumber than '80s sitcom reunions. They can't open doors. We need to clean the streets of the ones that are out there, let the others rot, think of their homes as big tombs. We'll turn parks into gardens and keep open the restaurants we like. Build a safe neighborhood around here."

People were nodding, on the computer screen and in the room.

"It's going to be ugly for a few weeks, but then it's our world. That is when we make the big changes."

"After you shoot people," Samantha said, almost under her breath.

"Nope, Sam. After I rescue my dog."

Faces lit up around the room.

"That's next. We're going to save all your babies next."

TEST

1. You may have noticed the intentional snub over the last two chapters of the which of the following words:

    A) Habberplabb
    B) Defenestration
    C) Cankle
    D) Pet

2. PETA's use of women in ads is:

    A) Embarrassing
    B) Sexist and misogynistic
    C) Transparent attempts at attention that fail to forward their cause
    D) All of the above

Chapter Eighteen

It was brutal. Mark carefully taught Emily, Chris, Bru-Dawg and two others to handle weapons. One of the anarchists decided to keep fighting with a shovel. It wasn't long before the sidewalk was difficult to walk on. *Slippery When Wet* was not just a Bon Jovi album title, it was the state of the sidewalk outside the mini-mall. It was a gray mess with sloppy chunks of brain and various parts of zombie mingled together. Screams of frightened pacifists from inside the mini-mall became the soundtrack as the group hacked there way through every zombie they could.

Mark took off laughing and Dani heard gunfire going up the street. It didn't take long until the rest of the zombies in the area had come groaning their way into the parking lot. Dani was just about to suggest they go back inside, regroup, and rearm when they heard a siren.

Dani's heart was gripped by fear. The same dumb fear that came over her whenever she was speeding and saw a cop driving in her rear-view. She assumed that all the cops had been long gone, turned into flesh hungry zombies. Dani looked around the lot. What kind of trouble could they get in for killing a couple dozen zombies?

The five zombies in the entrance to the parking lot turned around toward the sound. All five faces turned in time to be struck by a giant red fire truck. The zombies smashed under the huge truck, Chris was the first to laugh. The siren went off and the truck reversed and

127

crushed the remaining zombie parts into pulp. Mark waved from the driver's seat.

Mark tooted the fire truck horn and turned the truck around to drive into the parking lot. He had spray painted VEGAN POWER under the front windshield. Now everyone laughed as the truck rolled into the lot.

"I think this will work better than the Prius."

It took about an hour to secure the huge M-60 machine gun to the back of the fire truck on its tripod. Mark was the person who felt most comfortable shooting it. It sounded like thunder and had a 7.5 magnitude style kickback. Chris drove. Dani and Bru-Dawg lined the back of the fire truck with AKs ready to add fire power when needed. Emily held down the fort at the mini-mall and one of the anarchists followed in a Honda Element.

They had made a list of all the loved ones, humans and non-humans, in the area that they needed to gather. The first stop, however, was Dani's call. Magik's house.

The truck pulled out on to the street and they drove the wrong way on a one-way street for the hell of it. The sun was on its way down, fires had popped up around town but there were less screams. They didn't see many zombies until they passed through the Hawthorne shopping district. Five zombies had gathered behind the glass window of a taco place. The zombies couldn't figure out how to open the door so they kept the truck going. A block later they saw four zombies on the street.

Chris ran over one, dragging him for half a block as he turned the big red truck around. The other three lifted their arms and yelled at the truck. They were the first source of food these zombies had seen.

"Ahhhh!" times three.

Chris pulled the truck slowly past the zombies. Mark hummed the score to the *Rambo* movies as the back of the truck pulled up on the zombies. Dani and Bru-Dawg hurried to put on their sound-deafening earphones.

Mark loaded the first rounds into the mighty gun with a snap. The gun spit thunder and tore up the street in a line of spraying pavement chunks. It ate its way up the street until the fire shredded the zombies. They broke apart into pieces, hit by a dozen bullets. It was a safe bet one bullet destroyed each of the zombies brains. Bottom line was they were not getting up.

Smoke rose from the massive gun.

Mark turned back to Dani. "Maybe we should save this one for large groups."

Dani picked up the walkie talkie on her belt. "Keep moving, we're almost there."

The truck pulled ahead and they followed the directions Dani had given them. As they reached the block, Dani experienced her first real grief since the morning. She had been busy organizing. It was Magik she missed, but the whole world too. She hadn't liked people, she didn't like the world in general. Now that it was gone, here on a street that was practically her home, she felt the first remorse for all the things gone forever.

Cable TV, sports, schools K-12, college, public transportation, road repairs, the DMV, taxes, voting, shopping, and on and on. The list was endless. A small group of survivors would have to decide in the coming days which of these marks of civilization were important or worthy enough to rebuild. It wasn't just her love that Dani was mourning, but the simple life that was over. Dani choked up and hoped Mark didn't see her fighting back tears.

The fire truck pulled up into the drive way and Dani let the tears roll as she saw Crom stand in the window on top of the couch. He barked over and over and she could tell his voice was hoarse from two days of barking. Dani stepped off the truck. She walked toward the house and allowed a smile as she got closer to the front door. She got out the keys that Magik had given her.

"Ahhh!"

Multiple zombie voices called from behind the Harrison house. Dani put her hand up to signal Mark. The Juggalo family marched around the corner. Their various Insane Clown Posse shirts were stained in blood and gut chunks. Juggamom waddled her way toward Dani, and in some ways she looked healthier than before.

"Ahhh dude. I fucking hate Juggalos. Dibs on shooting them," said Bru-Dawg.

The anarchist got out of the Element with his shovel. "Oh come on, let me have at least one."

"No way, dude. Mark didn't let me shoot the neon guy, I have to shoot a Juggalo . . ."

Dani left Bru-Dawg making his case that he deserved to shoot the Juggalos. Dani opened the door to the house and Crom ran over to her. There was pee on the kitchen floor and he had pooped in the living room corner. He had dug at the carpet to try and cover it up. Dani got low and gave him pets as his tail wagged like a high speed windshield washer. Crom licked her face.

"You hungry boy?"

They had food waiting in the Honda. Dani grabbed the leash by the door when she heard the machine gun fire. She stepped out into the yard pulling Crom with her. Bru-Dawg and Mark laughed as Bru-Dawg swung the shovel at one of the zombie kid's head.

Dani cringed. "What the fuck?"

Bru-Dawg and Mark looked at each other confused.

"Fucking zombies?"

"Yeah, well I knew those idiots. Let's try not to enjoy it."

That was going to be hard, not enjoying this. Dani hated so many people three days ago. She was a raging misanthrope. It was hard not to feel cathartic release when shooting zombies.

"Dani, I just shot a Juggalo, don't be a buzz-kill," Bru-Dawg laughed.

Dani lead Crom into the Honda. Mark jumped down from the fire truck.

"Yeah come on, I can tell you hated all these people too, Dani."

Dani climbed back up on the fire truck.

"Magik said you hated yuppies."

Dani held her rifle in her lap. "Yeah, I do."

Mark put his hands out. "See, just think of the joy of cleaning up The Pearl."

The Pearl was Portland's downtown upscale neighborhood of high rise condos and art galleries. Dani hated walking through that neighborhood with a passion. Dani hadn't considered downtown, but if they were going to secure the city on both sides of the river they would have to deal with downtown.

"Yeah I suppose."

Mark got on his radio. "Hey there Bandit this is Screaming Wolf, were ready for the next address."

"Tomorrow we hit The Pearl."

TEST

1. The thing Bru-Dawg will miss most about civilization is:

    A) Cheap burritos joints

    B) Organized air travel

    C) Japanese DVD reissues of canon films

    D) Eye doctors

2. The thing Dani will miss most about civilization is:

    A) The postal system

    B) Libraries

    C) Independent Film Channel

    D) Disco roller rinks

Chapter Nineteen

The neighborhood around the mini-mall had several old, large homes and every single one of them would be needed. Once they had gathered the survivors, they had well over three hundred people and twice as many companion animals. Almost two thousand had checked in from around the city. It was an ugly task, but Dani led an effort to clear homes in the surrounding neighborhood.

Open a door, find all zombies, shoot zombies, double check the house and assign it to someone. Mark spent the first day finding guns around town. By then a cop and an Iraq-war-veteran-turned-radical helped give shooting classes to the people willing to do the house cleaning. Pyres sprung up to burn the bodies and with a lot of team work, the neighborhood got a post-zombie-apocalyptic vegan makeover.

The Red and Black and Hungry Tiger were opened for lunch and dinner, but money was no longer good for anything but wiping up zombie guts. Even though they talked about going downtown, it was a week before anyone really considered it. Mark and Chris had taken the fire truck and a passenger van through on day three to free and transport what survivors they found. The zombies were out in full force.

Mark stood on the roof of a five-story warehouse two blocks west of the mini-mall. Through his binoculars he could see the empty top of the Burnside Bridge. Mark and a few others had made plans to skate the world famous skateboard park underneath the bridge since day four. He could just barely make out the image of four zombies dragging their feet across the four lane bridge.

"They're crossing the bridge now."

Dani grabbed the binoculars. Mark smiled at her. The week spent dealing with the zombie apocalypse had changed her. She had hardened like a dog turd under a heat lamp. Dani wasn't positive she liked the new version of herself, but she was doing what she needed to do. Brent and his *With Zombie* novels seemed like a life time away. In reality, less than a week had passed since she was red-penning those books sitting across from Sally.

She could see the four zombies walking across the wide, flat bridge. Dani looked further down and saw something far worse. They didn't have signs and they were slightly better dressed, but a crowd that looked like a protest march came across the bridge at a turtle's pace. A soft, cold wind that came down from Alaska blew through her hair. The smell of a thousand dead zombies on a dozen pyres tickled her nose.

The wind suddenly changed. A more powerful blast blew northeast ,straight out of the Columbia River Gorge. It carried the smell of the pyres and all the survivors across the river right into downtown. It took the stupid dead fuckers a couple days, but they were making their way across the river into the V-district, driven by the smell of survivors carried on the wind.

"We can't wait. We need to clear downtown."

"Yuppies, my dear."

Mark put his arm around Dani. It felt odd and her gut reaction was to tell him to move his fucking arm. The reality was after days of zombie house cleaning, Dani needed a hug. The arm felt good. It was comforting to feel even the slightest affection.

Dani stopped him and put her arms around him. "Just a hug, OK?"

Mark nodded. "Whatever you need."

***

Mark drove the Prius behind the fire truck. Chris drove the truck. He was dressed in football shoulder pads and a Baltimore Ravens football helmet. On day two a crew spent a few hours in the garage building a steel ramming wedge on the front of the truck. Day three saw the addition of an eight-foot steel jousting bar. Dani sat in the back of Prius, enjoying the Slayer soundtrack for the first time. She cleaned her AK with a rag as they turned the corner onto the Burnside Bridge.

The crowd of one hundred or more zombies reacted at the sight of them. "AHHHHH!" times one hundred.

Mark looked at Dani in the rear view mirror as she sat up and loaded the first round into the firing chamber. Dani saw worry on his face. She turned around and saw a red Honda Civic speeding toward them on Burnside Avenue.

"I see it. Fucking Samantha and the Gandhi brigade," said Mark.

Dani picked up her radio and called to the fire truck. "Samantha is coming behind us."

The radio crackled, *"She is gonna love this."*

The fire truck roared as it sped across the bridge, and the battering ram hit the zombies first. There was a sound of a large smack and the zombies exploded into slime. Now experienced in zombie ramming, Chris perfectly timed turning on the windshield wipers. The wipers beat back and forth, clearing the gray zombie sludge from the window. Four zombies were speared by the jousting bar. None of them were dead, and each one reached out and groaned as best they could.

The Prius' sunroof opened and Dani stood up. The fire truck kept on its ramming mission. The zombies that avoided fire-truck-crushing turned on the Prius. Mark put the car in park. Dani felt him stand with his back to hers. Her heart beat out of control, but the steady calm Mark projected helped her relax. They both fired endless rounds, picking apart zombie after zombie as they ran toward the car.

Like shooting fish in a barrel? No, they would never do that. Dani tried to think of another, more vegan-friendly analogy as she fired away.

Out of the corner of her eye, Dani could see the red Civic parked safely at the end of the bridge. Dani didn't have time to be annoyed with Samantha right now. The zombies kept coming. Dani had to load a second clip and then suddenly she had no targets in front of her. Just a decaying pile of machine gun shredded zombies.

Dani turned around in time to see Mark shoot the last three zombies walking toward him. The last one tripped over the pile of the fallen dead before Mark directed his final shot to the zombie's head. The fire truck turned around. The steel jousting pole now had six zombies speared like a kabob.

Mark dropped into the seat and drove them closer. Dani saw Samantha's car move toward them since the zombie threat was almost gone. The Prius pulled up on the zombie kabobs. The kabobs still reached out and kicked their feet.

The red Civic pulled up behind them. Blocked by a zombie limb roadblock, Samantha honked her horn over and over.

Chris put the fire truck in park and leaned out the driver side. "Fuck you!"

Samantha stood up behind the mush of zombies. "What is wrong with you people?"

Dani laughed and walked toward the zombie kabob. It was a cross-section of Portland. Two hipsters were skewered closed to the front. One wore a bike helmet and a faded Earth, Wind and Fire shirt. The second was in a flannel shirt with rolled-up sleeves and the mandatory Portland beard. The next zombie in the kabob was a woman in roller skates with tall socks, and covered in traditional multi-colored tattoos. She must have turned zombie on a way to a roller derby game.

All the trends that drove her nuts about hipsters were skewered on the front of the vegan power fire truck. The closer she got, Dani found herself laughing hysterically. She couldn't believe the insanity of the moment she found herself in.

"There is a non-violent solution." Samantha looked for a way to walk around the zombie mush. "There is a doctor in Florida who is working to teach them."

Mark laughed. "Yeah right. I read that post on the Vegan Freak message board. There is no proof of that."

"You assholes don't want to find a solution. You're enjoying all this." Samantha had a desperate sound to her voice.

Dani looked up at Chris in his football helmet and shoulder pads. It would be hard to argue otherwise. Dani knew that she and the misanthropes among her were all too eager to take part in zombie removal. Dani walked back toward Samantha. There was nothing between them but an ocean of zombie pus.

"You want to stop us, you're going to have to get your hands dirty."

Samantha pointed. "Murderers!"

Mark and Dani got back in the car. Dani stopped at the door. "We're headed to yuppie town if you change your mind."

Two hours later . . . Samantha's Making Sense Interlude.

"Ah, negative on that back-up, it's under control." Mark looked up at Dani. Her focus was tight on the zombie walking toward her. It wasn't moving fast—it dragged one foot like most of them did. This guy was not as purple and decayed as most.

"Oh man, this guy wants his brains."

Dani jumped up onto the roof of the car and then onto the sidewalk. She came up so quickly on the zombie as he turned to follow her. Dani sprayed AK fire back at him without looking. Sure, she wasted a few rounds in the dude's chest but his head went *pop*. She opened the door to the condo building. The domino zombies on the bottom ate from the zombie on top of them like a cannibal train.

The top zombie groaned but didn't have the strength to stand.

Dani put her foot on the door to push it open and squeezed her AK.

"Wait!" The sound of the voice, was like a needle scratched across a full length LP. Dani turned around and saw Samantha of the Abolitionist Voice Committee. "Don't shoot Dani!"

"I am so not in the mood for an ideological discussion right now."

"If we intend to create a new world, we have to leave behind the madness of the old."

Dani watched over her shoulder as Mark marched toward them. "Sam, I don't think we have much of choice about that whole leaving the old world behind thing."

"We're vegans, and we need to find a non-violent solution, as the professor once said . . ."

"Goddamn it, Sam!" Mark yelled as he marched toward them. "Why don't you protest those PETA humane death camps and leave us alone."

"I admit," Samantha said, and turned to address Mark, "the moral bench mark is a little grayer since . . ."

"Since the dead started walking and eating people's brains," Dani pushed the door open and sprayed machine gun fire into the lobby of the building. The top zombie shredded into zombie crumbles before the two underneath it stopped squirming. Samantha screamed, Mark laughed and Dani closed her eyes. She should have enjoyed this, you know, shooting yuppies.

Samantha cried and pointed. "They were people, just like you once."

"Yeah well I changed in time." Dani slung the rifle over her shoulder and walked beside Mark toward their car.

"What happened to compassion? What happened to you Dani?"

Dani looked at her shaky hands. Her sense of humor melted away, her anger and sorrow suddenly felt misplaced. They had all lost so much

"Did you try to find another way?" Samantha grinned.

Dani shook her head and looked at her feet. "No, I suppose I didn't."

"Nope, you just went right to the quickest most violent path," Samantha continued "As liberationists it's disgusting that we have been so focused on our freedom, our survival. You've been missing the point since day one."

Dani looked at Mark. She could see sorrow and guilt in his eyes for the first time. Dani had hated Samantha since the first moment they spoke. Sam's ridged commitment to ideology without thinking for herself. It drove Dani nuts, but she had to admit Sam was right about a lot of things. Dani turned her back to Samantha and looked Mark in the eyes.

"She is right, as a species we treated this planet as if it was ours. Like our survival, our taste buds were all of more importance than any of the negative impacts."

Samatha nodded. "It's like Professor Fonzie says ..."

Dani put up her hands. "Don't push it, Sam." Dani put her arm around Mark. "We can't be that selfish. We need to forget about ourselves for a moment. Tell me, Mark, what do you want?"

"Animal liberation," said Mark.

Dani nodded. "When do you want it?"

Mark laughed. "Now."

TEST

1. One struggle one fight:
A) Rock and roll all night (party every day)
B) Human freedom, animal rights
C) Get those zombies out of my sight
D) Where it Went and Burning Fight

2. The funniest thing about the apocalypse:
    A) Rehabbing vehicles for ramming
    B) Mandatory mohawks and shoulder pads
    C) Using money to wipe ass
    D) Dropping things off tall buildings randomly

Chapter Twenty

Chris dropped the bloody football helmet on the floor of the mini-mall. Mark piled up the empty AK magazines but was too tired to consider filling them back up. A barbeque had broken out in the park across the street. They could hear a band playing and smell the tofurky cooking from blocks away as they rolled in. Emily and Chris sat down on a couch they had dragged into the garage after the space became a meeting area.

Mark sat down with them. "We need to have a talk," Mark said and looked at the ceiling out of exhaustion.

Dani sat down on the floor in front of them. "We're leaving in the morning. We realized there is something we forgot to do."

Emily and Chris looked at each other. "Yeah, I know what you're thinking." Emily pulled out a folder filled with papers.

Dani opened the folder and looked at the information. It was like Emily read her mind.

"There are groups back East and in Canada already starting to do this," said Chris. "We're planning on leaving too."

"We could split up the list."

Chris and Emily nodded.

"What about Portland?"

"Sarah, the grandmother from NW Veg, well she doesn't actually have grandkids, everyone just thinks she does," Emily laughed. "Anyway, she is taking charge. There is a United Airlines pilot who lived in North Carolina. It took a couple days to get organized, but he is gonna start flying people in."

Dani had read online about a caravan driving up the coast from San Diego, another from Colorado. Sarah had already started organizing the restaurants and grocery stores in the area to operate collectively. Everyone seemed okay with the concept of mutual aid for the time being.

No other city or community had built itself back up so fast, so that was why there were people coming from all over. Sarah organized garden crews, bread bakers, tofu and tempeh makers. Her husband was an engineer and he worked to keep the power and the communication grid going.

Dani looked at Chris and Emily. "You coming back?"

"Yeah, as soon as we can." Chris said put his arm around Emily. "Portland is our home."

They could smell it a mile down the road even with the windows shut tighter than a rectally inserted corn cob. It was different from the rotting stench of zombie limbs and guts they had gotten used to over the last couple days. It was fecal. A million pounds of digested grains churned around and shat out into overwhelmingly enormous piles of waste. That shit would spend every second of the day slowly seeping through the soil into the ground water. Before the revolution, farm workers pushed the unused manure with hoses into giant pools of unearthly dung. Unspeakable poop-thulu monsters lurked at the bottom of farms across North America.

The sun had just poked over the horizon as Dani and Mark pulled up to the first address on the list. A so-called local dairy, this field of ankle-deep shit was home to twenty thousand ladies who were forced into pregnancy every two years. Lactating was their business. After giving birth, she had only a day with her children. If they were boys they went off to become veal chops. Girls went back into the cycle. Welcome to milk business.

The cows closest to the fence stared at the Prius as it drove up to gate of the farm. They looked tired and weak. The women of this farm moved slowly—they weighed several hundred pounds more than the biggest humans.

"You were right about the gas masks," Dani said as she put the freaky-looking mask over her head.

"I wish I wasn't." Mark put on his mask. He had it since the '99 WTO protests in Seattle, and told Dani that his ex-girlfriend wore the one she had when they were gassed at a World Bank protest in D.C. They stepped out and walked to the gate. There was a chain and a padlock that held it shut. Mark pulled out his Glock, Dani covered her ears. He shot the lock and broke the silence of the rural Washington State morning. Birds flew away screaming as the blast echoed for miles.

They walked into the milking barns. A thousand pumps lined the long building, an assembly line. Each of these ladies was expected to produce more than eighty to one hundred pounds of milk a day until their bodies gave out, usually that only took four years. Considering the fifteen to twenty-year life span of a cow, it enraged Dani just thinking of it.

"Ahhhh!"

Mark lifted his glock at the familiar sound.

A zombie walked out of the dairy barn. It wore muck pants strapped over each shoulder and a face mask. Behind the mask his face rotted faster than most in the city. This zombie was starved and rotting alone.

"Get it over with," said Dani.

Mark walked up and put the pistol in the zombie's mouth, hoping to quiet the sound. The zombie bit down on the metal of the pistol just as Mark pulled the trigger. The pistol made a comically muted sound as the skull burst apart. The zombie fell with a thump. A cow directly behind them chewing on the last bits of dried soy bean meal at the bottom of the trough jumped back. She was locked in the huge pen with her black and white sisters. The shape of a thousand sisters filled the horizon almost as far as the eye could see.

The closest cow mooed at them. A chorus of moos broke around the nearest pen. Dani searched the dead zombie and found a key ring. She grabbed the keys and walked to the gate. The cows all stepped back, dozens stepping back together. They were unsure of her intentions, one of the cows sniffed the air. Their legs were covered in shit, and they could not move easily. Across the road an overgrown field of grain waved to them under the slight breeze.

Dani tried three keys before she found the right one. She opened the lock and swung the chain off. She threw it as hard as she could, smashing a milk pump inside the shed. Mark opened the gate wide. The first cow looked at Mark and then Dani. Her brown eyes were deep and filled with emotions.

"Go on now. You're free."

She stepped carefully, her front legs pulled out of the muck and she nervously stepped out into the area near the road. She looked past Dani at the milking shed. Dani felt her pain and suffering. Guilt over the suffering Dani's species had committed against her and her sisters twisted inside her.

"That's all over now. Go!"

Suddenly the large bovine took off like she had hit a line drive. Mark laughed as a stampede followed her. Some moved quicker than others. Three cows stood still in the rush around them to escape. One downed cow, dead for days, lay fifty feet from the humans. The cows mooed a final goodbye. One rubbed her nose on her fallen sister and then ran toward them.

Dani cried, even Mark had to lift up his mask and wipe away a tear.

"Where to next?"

"Already in the GPS."

Mark laughed. "Wonder how long those are gonna last?"

"I don't know," Dani said as she got into the driver's seat of the

Prius. "You think the international space station people are zombies now?"

They decided after that first farm that they wouldn't go until it got dark but the conditions were not good before collapse, and after they were worse than she imagined. Dani led them to the next farm on their list. The sign on the road said certified "Free-Range" eggs. Dani knew from her research on veganism that free-range was bullshit. No independent agency certified free-range and according to most states the bare minimum was required to claim it.

She also knew from the list Emily gave her that this farm had both full-on factory egg setup as well as the marketing tool of so-called *free-range* on the same land. They smelled the farm down the road. This time when they pulled up, they did see a few hundred chickens pecking around the yard. Dani followed the row of chickens back to a barn.

Across a long concrete slab a tiny hole in at the bottom was ejecting chickens.

"You're kidding me." Mark muttered.

"That tiny fucking hole in the wall is what makes them free range?"

Dani also understood that they would never have ventured across the concrete out of the little hole in the wall if they were not starved. Dani walked up to the barn and opened the door. The smell of ammonia was so strong she cursed and dropped the gas mask back over her face. All the chickens in this barn had to breathe that air without a mask, not only that but they lived in it. They breathed that foul gas into their lungs and it turned slowly into diseased flesh, which this farm packaged as a product to be eaten deep fried, in sandwiches or in salads.

Dani looked around the barn. Thousands of birds were still packed into six levels of hutches. Small conveyor belts rolled along ready to catch any eggs that slipped through.

Dani looked on the wall. A chart explained which hens and when they were forced into molting so they would produce more eggs. Dani ripped the calendar off the wall and felt stupid for her anger. It was over now, and these little ladies needed her help, not her anger. Mark walked in and cursed under his gas mask.

"Some of them will need down from the top levels."

They worked for almost two hours. Grabbing bird after bird and putting them down on the ground. The hardest part was finding so many that were already dead. Several had pecked each other or fought with other birds. Some had dehydrated, others starved. Most were missing the front ends of their beaks, as the free-range farms had chopped them off in hopes that they wouldn't peck each other to death. With the door propped open, the birds moved quickly out into the night.

The pain of finding the dead was hard, but the joy of seeing the others waddle out the door felt wonderful. The mix was an emotional see-saw. After working up a thick sweat and burning two hours of the night the free-range barn was empty.

Mark stepped out first and saw the white and yellow birds collect near a pond at the edge of the farm. Dani walked over to the grain silo. She knew many would not survive being feral. They would be open to predators, many didn't have the skills to survive but it was better that they try and fail. Anything was better than the life given to them before the collapse of the human race.

Mark had his mask up on his head. He stared at the large factory building further back off the road. The factory egg farm. "I don't know if I can handle this."

"We don't have a choice. Do you know what was said to me that made me decide I needed to be vegan?"

Mark shrugged.

"If it's murder in my head, I have to act like it's murder in my heart."

"Who said that?"

"I don't know, some young lady leafleting me. The point is,

Mark, that if we don't undo the mess here, no one will. We can't let all those birds die up there."

Mark nodded and walked up the hill toward the farm. They walked for a bit and suddenly they smelled a sour, rotting smell. A smell they knew all too well. Rotting death. Mark pulled out his Glock and held it out. They followed the smell to a large steel barrel the size of a Ford Explorer.

"Oh shit," Mark said and turned away.

Dani walked carefully up to the barrel and peeked over. She covered her mouth. Thousands of dead male baby chicks were piled up almost to the edge of the barrel. It was the cast away male chicks who would never grow up to be egg producing machines. A blood stained wood chipper next to the barrel was used to turn the chicks into "chick meal" which the farmers sold as fertilizer. Some farms fed them back to the chickens. It sounded too horrible to be true but here was the reality staring them in the face. It was feeding cows back to cows in feed that caused mad cow. What happened to the chickens when they ate their siblings?

Dani looked at the chicks in various stages of decomposition and something occurred to her. What did all these little dead guys have in common? They were killed for no other reason than being born male.

Dani had been a life-long feminist, dealing with the insult, "femi-nazi" from the first time she stood up for what she believed. She turned around and looked at all the female birds jumping over each other to get at the feed from the open silo. The pigs she released from the rape rack that afternoon who had been nursing babies through steel bars. Babies who, without the veganized zombie revolution, would have become hipster food. She thought about the cows she let out at the farm first thing this morning. Their only crime being born female in a species enslaved to serve humans. The very milk of their bodies stolen from them and taken to feed people of another species in far away places.

They were sisters all.

Mark tapped her on the shoulder. Dani nodded and they headed into the house of horrors. She knew there would be thousands of them. She opened the door and gasped. The smell, the sounds were over whelming. She flipped a switch and the lights clicked on with a massive buzz. As far as the eye could see, thousands of birds screamed for help. The cages were the width of a computer monitor and not much taller. Each one was packed so full of birds that they couldn't extend their wings. The conveyor belts still spun. After days of being ignored, they were covered in crushed eggs.

The smell of fecal matter and death danced around Dani's nose until she pulled the mask over her face. Maybe fifty percent or more of the birds were already dead and gone. There would be no more sleep tonight. Dani had to accept that they couldn't save them all. Long after the meat eating world of old had killed itself off these birds would still suffer.

Dani felt like dropping to the dirty floor and crying. Bawling her guts out at the inhumanity that caused this holocaust. Worse than a holocaust, a genocide ends in death. If the zombies hadn't come it would have kept happening, generation after generation of living beings bred into a cycle of slavery and exploitation. Genocide and slavery were not strong enough words. She would have to live with this nightmare in her memory the rest of her days.

Mark grabbed her shoulders. His voice muffled by the mask. "Dani, wake up." He saw her tears under the gas mask.

"We can't ever let this happen again, Mark."

"We have to get started."

Dani shook her head. "Promise me we won't let this happen again."

"Of course, it's over. That world killed itself."

Dani nodded. She turned around to the first cage. There were three dead hens lying inside the wire mesh, two still alive. The bird closest to Dani lifted her feathers in a sign of attack. Dani wrenched the cage open, it made a awful scratching sound. The hen screamed at Dani and jumped out. Mark had to get out of the way as the hen sped into the night. The last hen in the cage cowered. Dani reached in and pulled her out. On her arm she felt the stiff body of the dead.

The hen looked up at Dani. There was fear and pain in her tiny eyes. Her feathers were almost gone, shed in fear long ago. She was a pathetic looking featherless thing. Dani wanted desperately to hold her, and comfort her. The sound of thousands of other birds calling out for her help reminded her that she couldn't. Dani put the hen down.

Mark moved quickly—he had opened fifteen cages in the row behind her. This was true horror. Dani accepted a cold reality; she could shoot a thousand zombies before she would want to relive this experience. The hardest part was she knew they had years before this job would be done. Cleaning up the mess meat eating had made of the world was now her full time job.

TEST

1. You can do something to end suffering and exploitation of animals used in the production of meat, dairy and and eggs by:

> *A) Writing a big check to an animal welfare organization*
>
> *B) Playing a mouth harp on the porch with Grandpa*
>
> *C) Pooping in a wallet, putting it on the street corner and laughing at people when they pick it up and look inside*
>
> *D) Living a vegan lifestyle and advocating for the abolition of animal slavery*

2. Things that will not be missed from the old world:

> *A) Christmas sweaters*
>
> *B) The International Curling Federation*
>
> *C) New episodes of Two and a Half Men*
>
> *D) Subway five dollar foot long commercials*

Epilogue

Dani sat up in her bed. The great effort was only rewarded with a view of the overcast sky. The heater had kicked on but it wasn't that cold outside. It was October and the rainy Oregon fall was just tapping on her window to remind what was on the way. If she made it through this winter, it would be her last. Dani pulled her gray hair back and looked at her wrinkled feet. That was the problem with living four years shy of one hundred. You had to watch your body turn white and blue all over.

"Miss Dani?"

A young woman's voice followed a gentle knock. Young—ha—she was in her thirties and a doctor. The woman walked in wearing sweatshirt, looking casual except for the stethoscope around her neck.

"The night nurse told me you refused oxygen."

Dani took a deep breath. It hurt and it didn't come easy, but slowly the air filled her lungs. "She said I needed it to live?"

"That's right."

Dani laughed the painful old lady laugh and used the night stand to push herself up to the walker left at her bedside. "Don't you think I've lived long enough?"

"You're the last one . . ."

"All the more reason." Dani looked at the young woman. Her name was Amanda, her father made almond milk in the northeast part of town, kept the medical school well supplied. Her mother ran a school nearby. She had long curly blonde hair and the same blue eyes her father had. It made her thirsty for some of his chocolate almond shakes.

Dani smelled cooking oil, and the strong smell of cooking potatoes. She was about to ask if they were having fries with lunch when she saw the yellow school bus pull up. Some things didn't change. School buses may run on reused vegetable oil but they were still ugly and yellow.

"Who is that?" Dani pointed out the window.

"You don't remember?"

Dani shook her head.

"We talked about it yesterday."

Dani shrugged.

"My mom's history students."

Dani sighed and moved the past the doctor. The doctor kept talking. "You are a very important person and . . ."

Dani didn't listen, just walked out the bedroom door. "I know everyone wants a piece of me before I die. Get in fuckin' line." Dani sat in the lift that brought her down to the bottom floor. The doctor ran down the hall. Dani looked at her sweat suit. "You know before the revolution, doctors would only wear that to exercise in."

The chair hummed as it rolled down the stairs. The doctor walked behind her on the steps. "Just talk to them. They want to know what it was like and you can't blame them."

Dani pushed the stop button at the bottom of the stairs and looked at the young doctor's face. She had never known a world with hamburgers. Never known a world with rodeos, elephants in circuses, or products tested on animals. Sure, there were a few renegades out there, rumors of a cattle ranching out in Wyoming twenty years ago. Dani and Mark searched. They found great wild herds of quickly adapting cattle. Many didn't survive but the few who had thrived. They adapted quicker than the chickens, who seemed only to survive better in the Deep South.

This young woman only knew this world.

The front door opened and children burst in. They laughed and ran into the living room looking for spots to sit themselves down. They were between five and ten-years-old, it was hard for Dani to tell anymore. She looked at Amanda, and if looks could kill Dani would be filling out a toe tag.

Dani muttered under her breath. "You know how I feel about children."

Amanda raised an eyebrow. Maybe she didn't know. Dani and Mark had led a movement to keep people from breeding after the revolution. They were dismissed as misanthropes. It was the second community dividing debate after the great soy vs. rice milk throwdown.

In the end, Portland became a breeder town, Chicago did not. Despite the difference in ideology, after years on the road cleaning up factory farms, Mark and Dani wanted to come home to Portland, even if part of their mutual aid efforts went to maintaining schools.

Dani put her walker on the floor and walked toward the children.

Chicago kept going for several years but now it was like Atlanta, DC, Baltimore, Albuquerque, Phoenix. All those cities that rotted away with fifty story sky-scraping tombstones. Here lies civilization. It had been Dani's hope that all cities would fall.

Vegan survivors rebuilt. Portland suddenly became a world capital over night. L.A., New York, Chicago, Munich, London, Buenos Aires, to name a few, rebuilt slowly and surely. The survivors were few and far between but enough to build something new. It was better, but far from perfect.

Amanda's mother, the teacher, clapped her hands and got everyone's attention. She introduced Dani. One of the revolutionary pioneers, zombie killer, animal liberator, yadda yadda. Dani moved her dentures around as she sat on the pad in her walker. She could tell the kids were a little creeped out by her.

"Boo!"

The kids jumped in their seats then everyone laughed.

"You got some questions for the creepy old lady?" Dani askedwith a devilish grin.

"What happened to all the zombies?"

Dani looked at the teacher. *What the fuck do you teach these kids in history class?* She thought but just smiled at the little boy who asked. "Well they were dead, so the ones locked in houses and buildings just rotted away as if they were in coffins. The ones on the loose, well, didn't you guys talk about this in class?"

The kids nodded together.

"It wasn't exactly the best time of my life."

"Are you the last survivor left?" one of the girls asked.

Dani laughed. "I may be. In Portland I am."

"What was it like before the revolution?" a boy asked.

"I don't know how to answer that. A lot of people thought they were happy but that happiness came with a price. People just used things and rarely thought about where they came from or who it hurt to make the stuff. Those people were not any happier than we are." Dani looked at the faded, ancient tattoo on her arm. She got it when she first lived in Portland all those years ago. That was before she started thinking about the origin of her food, clothing, electronics. She thought back to the moment she decided to give up all those things she thought she needed. Dani laughed. The kids didn't know why she was laughing.

"Any of you kids know the word vegan?"

They looked at each other confused.

Dani smiled. "I suppose you wouldn't know that word, would you." Dani closed her eyes and took in a deep breath. "Good for you."

THE FINAL EXAM

1. Being vegan is easier than you might think. The key to successful vegan lifestyle transition is:
 A) Support from people who have done it before
 B) A healthy, balanced, whole food diet—in other words, don't be a potato chip vegan
 C) Don't ever think of your diet as limited—most new vegans expand the variety of foods they eat
 D) All of the above

2. When you finish reading this book, the fact you will never forget is:
 A) The tongue is the only muscle in the human body attached at one side
 B) The city of Portland, Oregon was named after a coin toss in 1844
 C) Jeremy Robert Johnson, author of Siren Promised, once gave himself a headache by trying unsuccessfully to sneeze with his eyes open
 D) Despite being terrible at math, David Agranoff, the author of this book, knows for a fact that $111,111,111 \times 111,111,111 = 12,345,678,987,654,321$

Author Afterword

At the time I wrote this novel, I had been Vegan for more than seventeen years. I take the issues involved with that choice very seriously, but hey, if you can't laugh at yourself, is it fair to laugh at others? This is my first novel attempt at satire. Not all of my work is this political, but very little of it comedic. I want to keep exploring our world and the nature of life through fiction. I hope if you enjoyed this work you will check out my other novels and stories. I hope each one of them is a unique experience, and if you enjoyed this one, I hope we can do it again soon.

The first four months this book is for sale, all my proceeds will go to a non-profit I volunteer with called Try Vegan PDX here in Portland, Oregon. We don't dress up like cartoon animals and protest, we don't get naked and use sex to sell eating vegetarian. We don't point fingers and judge people. We simply provide people interested in veganism a mentor who can show them how easy it can be. We provide information and help.

For more information:

www.TryVeganPDX.com

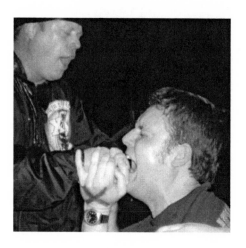

ABOUT THE AUTHOR

David Agranoff writes in several genres: Horror, Science Fiction, Fantasy and Bizarro. His first book *Screams from a Dying World* (Afterbirth Books, 2009) was nominated for a Wonderland Award for best collection. Agranoff has a novel coming soon from Afterbirth Books, *Hunting the Moon Tribe*, a cult bizarro kung-fu monster mash with a hint of erotic vampires set against a grand Wuxia Pan (Chinese Fantasy) adventure.

David lives with his wife, Cari, and their family of rescued rabbits in Portland, Oregon. He spent his childhood hanging out at the spaceport arcade in Bloomington, Indiana. He pays the bills by teaching autistic children in a high school and has been a strict straight-edge vegan longer than his students have been alive. In 2005, he spent 80 days in prison defending the 1st Amendment right to free association and belief. He watches *Commando* and Ching Siu Tung's *Duel to the Death* yearly and dreams of one day writing a licensed novel about Obi-Wan Kenobi, whom David thinks is a total badass.

You can "like" him on Facebook if you want updates on future books or follow his blog www.DavidAgranoff.blogspot.com

deadite press

You've seen Cannibal Holocaust. You've seen Salo. You've seen Nekromantik. You ain't seen shit!

Brain Cheese Buffet collects nine of Lee's most sought after tales of violence and body fluids. Featuring the Stoker nominated "Mr. Torso," the legendary grossout piece "The Dritiphilist," the notorious "The McCrath Model SS40-C, Series S," and six more stories to test your gag reflex.

No writer is more extreme, perverted, or gross than Edward Lee. His world is one of psychopathic redneck rapists, sex- addicted demons, and semen-stealing aliens. Brace yourself, the king of splatterspunk is guaranteed to shock, offend, and make you laugh until you vomit. *Bullet Through Your Face* collects three novellas demonstrating Lee's mind-blasting talent. Featuring "Ever Nat," "The Salt-Diviner," and "The Refrigerator Full of Sperm."

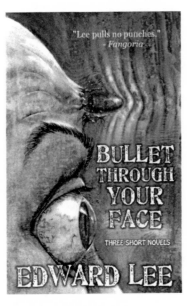

"Lee pulls no punches."
- *Fangoria*

BULLET THROUGH YOUR FACE

THREE SHORT NOVELS

EDWARD LEE

AVAILABLE FROM AMAZON.COM

"Squid Pulp Blues" Jordan Krall - In these three bizarro-noir novellas, the reader is thrown into a world of murderers, drugs made from squid parts, deformed gun-toting veterans, and a mischievous apocalyptic donkey.

". . . with SQUID PULP BLUES, [Krall] created a wholly unique terrascape of Ibsen-like naturalism and morbidity; an extravaganza of white-trash urban/noir horror."
- Edward Lee

"Apeshit" Carlton Mellick III - Friday the 13th meets Visitor Q. Six hipster teens go to a cabin in the woods inhabited by a deformed killer. An incredibly fucked-up parody of B-horror movies with a bizarro slant

"The new gold standard in unstoppable fetus-fucking kill-freakomania . . . Genuine all-meat hardcore horror meets unadulterated Bizarro brainwarp strangeness. The results are beyond jaw-dropping, and fill me with pure, unforgivable joy." - John Skipp

"Super Fetus" Adam Pepper - Try to abort this fetus and he'll kick your ass!

"The story of a self-aware fetus whose morally bankrupt mother is desperately trying to abort him. This darkly humorous novella will surely appall and upset a sizable percentage of people who read it... In-your-face, allegorical social commentary."
- BarnesandNoble.com

"Fistful of Feet" Jordan Krall - A bizarro tribute to Spaghetti westerns, Featuring Cthulhu-worshipping Indians, a woman with four feet, a Giallo-esque serial killer, a crazed gunman who is obsessed with sucking on candy, Syphilis-ridden mutants, ass juice, burping pistols, sexually transmitted tattoos, and a house devoted to the freakiest fetishes.

"Krall has quite a flair for outrage as an art form."
- Edward Lee

AVAILABLE FROM AMAZON.COM

CPSIA information can be obtained
at www.ICGtesting.com
Printed in the USA
FSOW02n1940011015
11771FS